I0450799

BEFORE I FOUND YOU

A De Courtenay Novella, Book Three

SHERRY EWING

Copyright © 2022 by Sherry Ewing

All rights reserved.

No part of this book may be reproduced in any form or by any electronic or mechanical means, including information storage and retrieval systems, without written permission from the author, except for the use of brief quotations in a book reviews.

Kingsburg Pres
P.O. Box 475146
San Francisco, CA 94147
www.kingsburgpress.com

Before I Found You is a work of fiction. Names, characters, places, and incidents are a product of the author's imagination. Locales and public names are sometimes used for atmospheric purposes.

Before I Found You first appeared in *Storm & Shelter*, the 2021 box set by the Bluestocking Belles and friends. Each of us used some of the characters belonging to other authors in our stories. The participating authors have given me license to publish this story as a stand-alone with their characters included.

Editor: Jude Knight
Front Cover Design: www.PeriodImages.com
Back Cover and Fonts: Sherry Ewing

Before I Found You/Sherry Ewing -- 1st ed.
ISBN eBook: 978-1-946177-59-9
ISBN Expanded Distribution Print: 978-1-946177-60-5
ISBN Amazon Print: 978-1-946177-61-2

Library of Congress Control Number: 202209631

A Quest Through Time (Book Five)

Promises Made At Midnight: The Knights of Berwyck,

A Quest Through Time (Book Six) - Coming July 2022

Regency

A Kiss for Charity: *A de Courtenay Novella (Book One)*

The Earl Takes A Wife: *A de Courtenay Novella (Book Two)*

Before I Found You: A de Courtenay Novella (Book Three)

Nothing But Time, *A Family of Worth: Book One*

One Moment In Time: *A Family of Worth, Book Two*

Under the Mistletoe

A Second Chance At Love

A Countess to Remember in *Desperate Daughters: A Bluestocking Belles with Friends Collection* (May 2022)

Learn more about Sherry's books on her website at www. SherryEwing.com/books

Join Sherry's newsletter at http://bit.ly/2vGrqQM

For Carol & Jude

I couldn't do all this without the two of you. Your friendship means the world to me. Thank you for all your love and support over the years!

And

To author Elizabeth Essex for her kindness in sharing her knowledge of all things nautical!

BEFORE I FOUND YOU

CHAPTER 1

Bath, England
February 14, 1815

Captain Jasper Rousseau surveyed the crowd, wishing he could be anywhere other than this ballroom full of Bath Society. Standing near the balcony door, he nodded to those who strolled past him, although he continued to wish for a hasty retreat. If past experience was anything to judge by, many of the *ton* gathered here tonight would look down on him. He may have enough wealth to be comfortable for more than one lifetime but, without a connection to a title, he was outside of their circle. Not that he really cared. He wanted their investment, not their approval. For the most part, the people in attendance at the Valentine's Day Ball were strangers but some had done business with him. Indeed, somewhere in this room might be the prospective investor he was meeting in the morning.

He caught his mother's eye from across the room and she offered him a small smile of encouragement. He had fulfilled his obligation to her by escorting her to this event. But he would rather be at sea with the planks of his ship beneath his feet instead of in a ballroom with a cravat twisted entirely too tight like a noose around his neck. At least Bath was in close proximity to tomorrow's meeting.

"Buck up, ole chap," a gentleman chuckled next to him. "This, too, shall pass."

Jasper steadied himself. He had not realized his face showed his feelings. "I was just admiring the dancing," he replied before turning his full attention to the gentleman. "Have we met?"

"Lord Adrian de Courtenay," the man said holding out his hand.

"Captain Jasper Rousseau," he replied as he shook the gentleman's hand. His soft French accent caused a flicker in the man's demeanor before he masked the look in a friendly smile.

"A pleasure," Lord de Courtenay said before he, too, surveyed the room. "You're not a regular at such an event, not that I blame you. These balls and rounds of the Season can be quite tedious."

"Which is most likely why I avoid them at all costs," Jasper chuckled as if jesting, although in all honesty that reply was not too far off its mark. He was only here because his mother insisted. His parents wanted grand-children. Jasper had yet to find someone who remotely interested him, let alone tempted him into marriage. He had plenty of time. He was, after all, only thirty. A ball, according to his mother, was just what Jasper needed. "Are you enjoying yourself this evening?"

Lord de Courtenay gave a small laugh. "More so than you, it appears. You look as though you are at a funeral instead of a ball."

"I suppose I have distanced myself from the revelry. My mother would no doubt be appalled." Jasper nodded once more to his mother across the room and plastered a smile upon his face for her benefit. "What about you?"

"I am here with my lovely wife," Lord de Courtenay said, discreetly pointing in the direction of a young blonde lady in a pale pink dress. She excused herself from the group of women she had been talking to and began making her way toward her husband.

"A reason to celebrate on such a special occasion," Jasper answered before taking a sip of his champagne. *Another damn happy couple. The room was full of them.*

Lord de Courtenay raised his own glass in a silent salute. "Plenty of women here would love the chance to dance, Captain Rousseau. Find someone to perform introductions to the lady of your choice and enjoy yourself." With a smirk of encouragement and a wave of his hand, he excused himself to meet his wife, taking up her hand and raising it to his lips.

Lucky man, Jasper thought before he looked about

the room once more. He supposed to please his mother he should make at least an attempt to enjoy himself and choose someone for the next dance.

A young woman suddenly caught his attention as she skipped to the lively patterns of the current dance. Dark brown hair was swept up in a pleasing coiffure sprinkled with what looked like diamonds winking in the candlelight of the room. Her gown was pale blue with a pink ribbon just below her breasts. She turned and the look on her face was one of bored indifference, making Jasper inwardly laugh. Had Lord de Courtenay seen in his features what this woman showed to any who cared to gaze upon her?

Jasper continued to view her from a distance. Blue sapphires hung from her ears while a delicate golden chain with the same stones and diamonds graced her neck. He continued to watch, a slow grin spreading, until the dance ended and she gave a small curtsey to her partner.

As she rose, she scanned the room and he briefly wondered whom she was looking for in the overfilled ballroom. Their gazes met and held for an instant on a heartbeat. Jasper raised his glass in a silent toast and her eyes widened before she looked away, leaving the dance floor and melting away into the crowd.

His curiosity roused, Jasper drained the rest of his glass and handed the empty flute to a passing servant. He began to move, casually walking among the throng of people, hoping to catch another glimpse of the young woman who had momentarily caught his attention. His taste did not normally run to young maidens. She could hardly be older than a score of years, he surmised, as he continued searching for her. There she was, near the banquet table.

She appeared thoroughly engrossed in the delicacies before her. She at last took a small slice of cake decorated with a heart and placed the treat on her dish. Jasper took a plate for himself and slowly made his way down the table until they stood next to one another. They reached for a fruit tart at the same time. A gasp escaped her as she mumbled an apology, snatching her hand away from the dessert. She looked up to stare at him, and her mouth opened in an O of surprise, though her eyes twinkled with delight. They stood staring at one another only for a moment, then she rapidly turned away from him.

A sigh escaped him. Under Society's protocol he must be introduced to a young woman before having a conversation with her. He turned around so they were back to back, knowing it was expected of him. He could sense she had not moved to distance herself from him. Was she, too, just as interested in knowing exactly who he was? He held back a smile.

"*Bonsoir, mademoiselle,*" Jasper pitched his voice to be heard over the music in the next room and other conversations intruding into their moment together. He swore he heard her breath catch in her throat and he waited to see if she would acknowledge him.

"Good evening to you, sir," she replied, her voice a breathy whisper. She set her plate down on the table as though filling it had been but an excuse to keep her occupied. His near empty plate joined hers and he noticed she had taken a small nibble from the slice of cake.

Jasper waved to a servant, who quickly moved forward to offer the tray he carried. Jasper selected two crystal flutes of champagne before he hesitantly held one of the glasses toward the lady behind him. Her gloved fingers briefly touched his when she accepted his offering and Jasper's heart raced at the contact. How could such a young miss prompt such an intense physical reaction? He didn't even know her name.

"Perhaps you would favor me with the next dance," Jasper said hopefully but, of course, she would decline.

"I am afraid I cannot," she answered and her tone sounded somewhat disappointed.

"Because we have not been formally introduced?" he asked, already knowing her answer.

"Yes," she confirmed before rushing onward, "I'm sorry."

"Perhaps we can find someone who could remedy the situation."

He waited. But instead of answering she placed her glass on the table, her fingers lingering on the crystal stem. He set his own glass down, their hands nearly touching. He swore he could feel the heat of her skin next to his own. He turned slightly to better see her.

She looked up over her shoulder. At first, he thought her eyes were a soft brown but after she blinked, he saw that they were, in truth, hazel. His gaze moved down to her parted lips, wondering how they would taste after the champagne she had sipped and the sweet cake she had eaten.

"That would be lovely," she finally answered. She blushed before looking away and Jasper had the urge to pull her into his arms. Not that he would ever embarrass her so. As they both turned to face the room a gentleman came and bowed before her, holding out his hand.

"I believe this dance is mine, M—"

"Y-yes, o-of course," she quickly stammered. As she was led away, she glanced back only once, to smile at Jasper before she once more disappeared into the crowd.

Jasper stood alone wondering about the identity of this mysterious young lady and who, exactly, would be able to introduce them.

CHAPTER 2

Miss Miranda de Courtenay was in turmoil and there was no one she could blame other than herself. She should have never begun to converse with a gentleman to whom she had not been introduced, let alone allowed such a lingering glance. But he had hypnotized her when he all but pulled her toward him with his dreamy green eyes.

Filled with thoughts of him, she missed a step in the patterns of the dance! She quickly caught up to her rightful place in line with the other women. She craned her neck around the room when she dared. Where had he gone and more importantly... who was he? Never had she felt such an instant attraction. And he felt the same, she was certain. Would he seek an introduction? Would he come calling? Perhaps he was a duke or a marquis! An earl, at least—her quest to wed only nobility had been engrained in her every action as long as she could remember.

Some of her actions to that end had been unfortunate, of course. Her horrible embarrassment during the Hollystone Hall fiasco came to mind before she quickly dismissed it. She had known the Grenford brothers were rakes, but she had never imagined they would flirt with a maiden like her without intending marriage.

An inner voice pointed out she had only just been forgiven for her part in the forced wedding of her brother and his wife. Adrian had overreacted. He and Celia had loved one another for years. Adrian should be grateful that Miranda had prevented Celia from falling into the clutches of the marquis who wanted her.

What did it matter that Miranda's motivation was to secure the man for herself? Everything had turned out for the best. For Adrian and Celia, at least. The marquis turned out to be a rake, as well. And how was a lady meant to tell, when these rogues were welcomed into polite society? It was hardly her fault if she continued to be attracted to the wrong men who only had one thing on their minds.

She moved down in the line and acknowledged the man before her as the dancers changed partners. She gulped back a sharp remark when she recognized the Marquis of Wyndham, the despicable man she had just been thinking about.

She dismissed the marquis with a toss of her head as the dance continued and the line moved onward and she was reunited with her original partner. She gave him a brief smile. She had found him attractive earlier in the evening. He was a viscount but, to be honest, that was all she could remember about him. Later, she would need to check the dance card dangling from her wrist just so she could remember his name.

The ending notes of the music echoed in the room and Miranda sank into a curtsey. At her claim she was parched, the viscount went to fetch her some punch, giving Miranda the opportunity to scan the room for the gentleman who had captured her attention. She saw him standing next to an older woman but the lady was unknown to Miranda so there would be no help with formalities from that direction. Still... he had such a commanding presence about him and she admired the dashing figure he presented in his evening finery. Surely, he must be titled.

No man had the right to look so handsome. Earlier, after she had dared to look up at him, she had come very close to reaching up to push back the lock of his blond hair that had fallen rakishly across his brow. She had done enough foolish acts in the past few years, but she had luckily not made a spectacle of herself tonight. That was the last thing she needed. Not when her brother Adrian had only tonight forgiven her for the role she had played in ensuring he wed his lady. Still... A total stranger had her tongue-tied. Never in all her twenty and three years had some man done that to her. What had come over her?

Her eyes followed him when he walked out the balcony doors and into the dimly lit night air. He casually sat back against the marble railing, folding his arms across his chest as though he had not a care in the world. Surely, he was silently asking her to join him. She began to move in his direction, hesitating briefly when the voice of reason demanded she remain indoors. It wouldn't be prudent to allow her heart to rule over her head. She was here to find a titled gentleman as her husband. But perhaps this mystery man of hers had all that she had been looking for. It was possible, was it not?

Right before she reached the doors, she wavered again and looked back into the ballroom. Adrian and Celia were dancing and only had eyes for one another. Even her sister Grace, with whom she had lived since her brother exiled her after his forced betrothal, was deep in conversation with her husband Nicholas. Surely, Miranda would not be missed for a brief moment or two. Throwing caution to the wind, she stepped forward into the shadows of the cool night.

She was not sure what to expect. Being outside alone with a man she did not know was a bold move. If she needed reinforcements, she could easily call out for help, but that would hardly do her reputation any good. It had barely recovered from her last scheme. Society's memory was short, remembering scandals only until something new came along for them to gossip about—or until something happened to remind them. She couldn't afford to give them new fodder to chew on.

She could not resist. Miranda took the remaining few steps until she stood next to him, and he rose to his full height, his hair tousled by the evening breeze. She suppressed the urge to push back the lock of hair across his brow that refused to stay in place. *Oh my, but the man was tall!*

Miranda did not even realize she offered him her hand until he leaned down and kissed the air between her knuckles. His fingers were warm even through the silk of her gloves. How would they feel if her hand was bare? Good heavens! What was coming over her?

"*Mademoiselle,*" he whispered in a husky French accent, causing goose bumps to rise on her arms. His voice was utterly divine!

"Miranda," she said offering only her first name. It was hardly appropriate, but she did not wish to see his disinterest when he learned she was a "Miss" and not a "Lady".

Although it might not matter. Many gentlemen present this evening were on the lookout for a well-dowered heiress to enrich their estate. The man before her could be one of them. Even though she could not attach "lady" to her name, she was still wealthy in her own right... or would be when she finally wed.

Love had nothing to do with what really mattered in life—marriage to a husband within the nobility, one with enough wealth to keep her and her children in luxury. Not for her a boring life as a country matron, with nothing to do or to talk about beyond counting sheets and breeding children. She wanted a glittering life as a Society hostess! It would be an adventure. Or so she had always thought, and she would not allow her heart to rule her head.

She bit her bottom lip before she realized she had done so. The man before her could not know it was an automatic reaction when she was worried. She watched his brow arch in surprise before a grin turned up at the corner of his lips.

"Jasper," he finally replied in return, examining her reaction to his touch. "The evening has become brighter now that you have joined me for a breath of fresh air. Look how the stars above beam in approval that they may gaze down upon you."

Miranda's lips twitched at the compliment. Very nice, though she sensed that he used this phrase often. She realized he still held her fingertips and she reluctantly pulled them away before waving her hand towards the crowd inside. "It's quite the crush this evening. Have you been enjoying the ball?"

"I am now," Jasper replied, leaning back against the marble railing again.

Miranda blushed at his words. Another well planned compliment, or so it seemed. Miranda was used to them. She had utilized them herself enough times in the past to grab the attention of men she had hoped to snare into marriage. Obviously, since she was still unwed, she had failed. Given her own distrust of his practiced charm, she might need to rethink her approach to wringing a proposal from the peer in her future.

She chanced another glance at him. He watched her intently. "I have not seen you join in with the dancing," she replied softly, before giving him a small smile.

The edges of his lips again crooked upward. He had guessed what her words meant; that she had been searching for him. "Maybe I have not found the right partner."

"There are plenty of women who would more than happily accompany you," she remarked, although a part of her was thrilled he had not danced with another. What would it feel like to dance the night away with him?

"And does that include you, *ma chérie?*" He took a step closer and once more reached for her hand, rubbing his thumb across its back. He pulled her slightly closer to his side and she could sense the slightest hint of his cologne. She inhaled deeply. A pleasant mixture of musk, spice, and something else she could not detect. It was intoxicating, and she swallowed hard at what this man was doing to her.

Silence stretched between them, even the distant melody of music from inside seemingly diminished in Jasper's presence. His eyes continued to work his magic on her, pulling her deeper under his spell. Her breath hitched in her chest and she suddenly found herself unable to breathe. She had done it again... made a horrible mistake. What had she expected when she met a mysterious man alone... in the dark... with all of Society but a heartbeat away?

He was waiting for her answer. She took a deep breath to steady her nerves. "I am afraid that would never do. We still haven't formally been introduced," she finally whispered, while she continued to gaze into those hypnotizing green eyes.

He raised her hand to his lips and kissed her hand. Miranda gasped at his boldness. "Maybe we should just give in to whatever is between us. Surely no one will notice one more couple upon the dance floor." He began gently pulling her toward the door leading inside.

She quickly tugged on his arm. "Good heavens, no!" she replied. "My brother would never approve."

Jasper gave a chuckle and the deep baritone caused her heart to flip end over end. "Brothers generally never do. Why do I sense you tend to try and bend your brother, and Society for that matter, to your will, *mademoiselle*?"

Miranda laughed but her tone sounded strained to her ears. His words were more accurate than she wanted to admit. "Why, you know nothing about me, good sir!"

He shrugged and continued escorting her inside by tucking her hand in the crook of his elbow. "Perhaps not, but let's enjoy our moment together with a dance," he urged softly, while the musicians struck up the chords as if he conjured them to do so for his own personal pleasure.

Miranda's eyes widened, listening to the tune that began in the ballroom. "But the next dance is a waltz!"

"Well... so it is. Dance with me, Miranda. Throw caution away and show the *ton* you care not for their restrictions," he coaxed, holding out his hand for her to take when they reached the edge of the dance floor.

The prudence engendered by the last few months in disgrace melted like snow in the heat of his gaze. She did not think nor did she hesitate when she placed her hand in his. He gently pulled her into his arms and she forgot everything else but Jasper. He swept her into the pattern of the waltz as though they had danced together a thousand times before.

Jasper's eyes twinkled in the candlelight of the room and Miranda could barely contain the smile that flowed effortlessly across her face. She'd had no way to calculate his social position before accepting, and somehow being held in his arms felt so very right. Perhaps she had found her match in this handsome unexpected gentleman.

As Jasper continued whirling her around, she noticed her brother stood at the edge of the dance floor with a frown. She recognized that look and knew the moment the dance ended, Adrian would whisk her away and send her back home with Grace. Her face fell, knowing her time together with Jasper was at an end.

"Someone so beautiful should have only a smile

reflecting in her eyes, *ma petite*," Jasper murmured, as they continued twirling around the room. "What troubles you so?"

"My rash decision to dance with you will not go over well with my brother. From the look he is giving me, he knows we haven't been introduced. I'm afraid I'll be escorted from the ball as soon as our waltz is finished."

"My apologies, Miranda, if I have caused you trouble. It wasn't my intention to damage your reputation."

"You are not entirely to blame, Jasper. I could have adhered to the rules that are expected of me," she replied. "I could have just as easily declined."

"I'm glad you didn't, but hope we can salvage the situation."

"I'm also happy I accepted the invitation to dance with you." She smiled up into his handsome face, regaining some of her confidence that Adrian would forgive her impulsiveness.

"I have a business appointment in the morning. Where can I call upon you or leave my card with your brother?" Jasper asked to the dying notes of the music.

Before she could answer, couples began withdrawing from the dance floor and she saw Adrian making his way towards her.

"I must go," she said quickly. "Thank you so much for the dance... Jasper."

"Miranda!"

She could not give in to her desire to have one last look at Jasper when he called out her name. She also wouldn't look back. She had turned her nose up at the restrictions of Society where he was concerned, and she would not make things worse.

She made her way towards her brother who said not a word but took her arm, escorting her to Grace and Nicholas who already held her redingote. Her time at the ball with her handsome stranger was over.

CHAPTER 3

Miss Miranda de Courtenay sat in the morning room sipping tea in Highgrove Manor remembering the gentleman she had met last night. He had been the stuff dreams were made of. His green eyes had held her spellbound when she had dared to dance with him... a waltz of all things. Her breath hitched with the memory of how she had wished to tame those blond locks back into place when they fell across his brow. And to be held in his arms while they made their way through the crowded dance floor... she had wished at the time that the music would never end!

Miranda glanced up when her sister Grace entered the room. One look upon her face told her much. Miranda was in trouble... again.

"You might as well just tell me what I did now and get it over with, Gracie," Miranda said with a heavy sigh before pouring her sister a cup of tea. Grace slid a newsprint across the table. The blaring words of *The Teatime Tattler* blurred before her eyes. "Oh, no!"

"Oh, yes," Grace answered before taking a sip of her tea as if this alone would make the latest gossip regarding her sister disappear. "Fortunately, the article is on the second page most likely because the charity ball was held in Bath and most of Society was in attendance."

Miranda opened the newspaper and scanned the lettering for what would obviously condemn her once again. She began to read aloud.

Gentle Readers:

After last night's Bath Valentine's Day ball, this reporter learned of a most tantalizing bit of gossip for your reading pleasure! A certain young lady, Miss M.d.C., was in attendance and it's been reported she has once more begun her search for a titled gentleman for a husband. Yet, despite the obvious rules amongst the ton, this reporter heard she danced with a gentleman whom she hadn't been introduced to. The music barely ended before her brother, the earl, had her escorted from the event. We'll have to wait to see if Miss M.d.C. is allowed at other events in the Season or if she'll be exiled to the country... again!

An Anonymous Reporter of
The Teatime Tattler

Miranda closed the newspaper not caring to read anything else that rag might have mentioned. "Well, I suppose it could have been worse," she said looking across the table at her sister.

"Adrian will be furious," Grace groaned.

"When is our brother not angry with me over some slight?" Miranda replied taking up her cup and saucer.

"You need to learn to control these outrageous notions that continue to flit into your head that you think you can get away with, sister," Grace fumed. "Society will be lenient for only so long before you're completely ostracized. You'll never find a husband if you can't hold your head up within Society."

"I can barely move among them as it is now due to my past schemes," Miranda said sadly. "Honestly, you'd think I was the only one who was prepared to do anything to catch a title."

"But you tend to get caught, my dear. There's a difference," Grace answered reaching over to take Miranda's hand. "I want you to find love, dearest sister. That is far more important than any title a man might have."

"You don't understand what it's like to be the only one in this family without one," Miranda huffed on the verge of tears.

"Maybe not but I do know a thing or two about being in love. Love will carry you through every heartache the world may throw at you. Don't be a fool to only look at the title and not the man whom you wish to wed."

Grace finished her tea and left Miranda to her thoughts. Marry for love? She scoffed at the idea. Love was for fools!

CHAPTER 4

J asper handed over the reins of his horse to a lad who came running to see to his animal. He gave the bay a pat on the neck before his steed was led away, leaving Jasper staring at the four-story brick mansion before him. At Lord Nicholas Lacey's urging, Jasper had ridden over to Batheaston and enjoyed the excursion, knowing their meeting was not far from his own country estate. Once the business portion of the day was concluded, Lord Nicholas offered to show him the rest of his property and perhaps also take in a bit of sport along the way.

As Jasper approached the door, the faint melody of someone on a pianoforte reached his ears. There could be no doubt that whomever was playing the instrument was accomplished. He rapped upon the door and waited only a fraction of a moment before it was opened. The butler stood back as Jasper entered the foyer.

"Captain Rousseau," the man said as he led him to the parlor. "His lordship is expecting you, sir. If you would await him here, I shall tell him you've arrived."

Jasper watched the man disappear quietly down the marbled hallway before he gazed around the parlor. It was richly decorated with mahogany furniture, the fabric of the chairs a deep shade of forest green. The curtains had been drawn back to let in the morning sun but it was the sound of the high soprano voice that caused Jasper to continue forward through to the next room.

The woman sat at the pianoforte with her back to him, not realizing she was no longer alone. A riot of dark curling hair tumbled down her back as if she had forgotten to finish her morning toilet in her eagerness to reach the instrument. Her white dress had small pink rosebuds scattered along the fabric while dainty slippers sat on the floor near her feet. The lady's nimble fingers flew over the ivory keys as if she had performed this song a hundred times or more, because there wasn't any sheet music to guide her. Her voice sang in perfect accord to the melody and, as her hands finished the song, the last strains of the melody faded away into the room. Lord Nicholas was a lucky man to have such an accomplished wife.

"My apologies for interrupting your morning, Lady Nicholas, but that was very well done," Jasper said, giving the well-deserved compliment to the performance he had been privileged to hear.

She quickly placed her feet into her discarded shoes. "You are mistaken, sir, I'm not..." She laughed and turned.

His eyes widened in surprise. "Miranda!"

Her hand went to her throat just as startled. "Jasper! Whatever are you doing here?" She quickly looked around the room as though for a missing chaperone, since they were completely alone.

His brow furrowed at the implications of this chance meeting. "*Bloody hell...*" he swore softly. He mumbled an apology before coming forward. How could he so misread the situation? He had been sure he and the lady before him had forged a connection. "You are the lady of the house?"

Miranda stood, placing a chair between them, looking as confused as Jasper himself was feeling. "What?"

What game had this woman had been playing last evening? He knew a few among the *ton* had open marriages but Jasper stayed clear of women who were only looking for someone to fulfill whatever needs their husbands lacked the wherewithal to supply... not that Lord Nicholas gave the impression that he lacked anything at all.

"Lord Nicholas..." he tried again, feeling sick that he had briefly coveted another man's wife. "He's your husband? Is this why you were so vague about your identity at the ball?"

Her eyes cleared and a joyful laugh escaped her. Jasper saw nothing comical about the situation.

"Nicholas isn't my husband, Jasper. He's my—"

"There you are, Captain Rousseau," Nicholas said, entering the room. "I see you've met Miranda."

Her eyes darkened, as though in disappointment. "Captain?" she asked, in a hushed whisper.

Jasper gave a short nod, before turning to shake Nicholas's outstretched hand. "Actually, the lady and I lacked formal introductions last eve." Jasper turned once more to look at the young woman before him. She had turned away while he had been shaking Nicholas's hand but, as she turned back to them, he swore he saw the remnants of tears lingering on her eyelashes.

"Then let us remedy the situation now," Nicholas beamed. "Miss Miranda de Courtenay, may I present Captain Jasper Rousseau. My wife Grace and Miranda are sisters."

Miranda curtseyed while Jasper bowed. "Captain Rousseau," she said, politely, but the fire of the woman he had met at the ball suddenly appeared dimmed.

"Miss de Courtenay... it's a pleasure," Jasper said before the name hit him. "Are you, perhaps, related to Lord Adrian de Courtenay?"

She nodded. "He's my brother. Have you met?"

"Only briefly, last evening."

Nicholas stepped forward, offering Miranda his arm.

"Grace was asking for you upstairs. I'm certain you won't mind if the captain and I leave your lovely company while we discuss business."

Miranda stole a glance at Jasper. *Ah... there she was...* His heart leapt at the flash of irritation that briefly lit her eyes. Clearly, she was annoyed at being politely dismissed from a discussion between gentlemen.

"Business? What kind of business?" she asked.

"Captain Rousseau has recently purchased a merchant brig called *The Legacy*. It's docked in London and we're to discuss shipping opportunities that will benefit us both," Nicholas replied as they reached the entryway and he walked her toward the stairs to the upper floors. "Nothing too exciting for such a lovely young woman; it would surely bore you to tears, Miranda, to hear all the details."

"Of course," she replied quietly. Her features stiffened into studied indifference. "I will see to attending Grace, then. Good day, Captain Rousseau."

"Miss de Courtenay." He gave a short bow and watched her head up the stairs to disappear out of sight.

He wasn't allowed any further time to contemplate the woman who had consumed his thoughts for the better part of last evening. Lord Nicholas led him into his study. A reminder Jasper was here on business and needed to keep focused on why he was at Highgrove Manor in the first place. He wasn't here to court a woman, not when he had a new ship to see to and accommodations to be made so he could also take passengers as an extra source of income. And untrustworthy rivals like the Danvilles, father and son, who had bid on *The Legacy* and lost her to Jasper, would love to steal his cargoes. He would leave thoughts of Miranda for another day. At least now he knew where to find her.

CHAPTER 5

Miranda paced the garden path that gave her a clear view of the front door. This morning, she had waited for what seemed like days, instead of hours, for the opportunity to speak with Jasper. When she heard Nicholas saying he looked forward to seeing *The Legacy* next month, she knew the moment was upon her. She flew through the manor to the kitchen and out the back door before she could rethink her actions. Now, with her shawl wrapped around her, she tried to forget about the cold and instead focus on what she really wanted... just one last moment with Jasper.

She should forget him, shouldn't she? Of all the wretched luck! A captain of a merchant ship was not in her plans, no matter how handsome he was. Who would have imagined that the first man ever to really spark her interest would have no title? She had wanted a title of her own since she was a small girl, especially since

Grace married their second cousin, the Earl de Court-ney, and became his countess. As the great grand-daughter of an earl, Miranda was not even an 'honorable'. Just a 'miss'. She wasn't going to be a Mrs., that was for certain. Even her brother was a peer now, inheriting the earl's title when Grace's first husband died. And Grace had gone on to marry the second son of a duke!

Miranda could not give up her dreams of being, at the very least, a countess. Or could she? She shook her head. Forget her dreams of marrying nobility? What a silly notion. A gentleman with a title would be lucky to have her as his wife. It was all she had ever wanted for her life.

She stomped her foot in frustration at the injustice of her situation! Being stuck out here in the country with Grace and her children left her little to no oppor-tunity to convince someone within the peerage to offer for her. Last night's ball would have been a prime opportunity to find her next conquest, but she had failed herself by getting smitten by a pair of mesmer-izing green eyes. What was she to do?

After she had seen Grace earlier, Miranda had watched from the upper window of her bedroom over-looking the courtyard as Jasper and Nicholas left for a short ride on their horses. Even remembering Jasper when he mounted that horse caused Miranda's heart to flutter in her chest. Both men had discarded their cravats but Miranda's gaze was focused only on one.

Her eyes had wandered down to the brief glimpse of blond hair at the opening of Jasper's shirt. Fingers tingling, she reached out to the glass pane window as though she could really feel his chest. She closed her eyes briefly as she imagined the texture of his skin. When she opened them again, their eyes met and his smile was truly wicked.

Miranda had jumped back from the window as though burned. How could Jasper be even more handsome in broad daylight than he had been in the candlelight at the ball?

Which, of course, was why she was standing here in the cold waiting for him to leave the manor. She blew air into her icy hands and was just about to give up on this idiotic notion when the door opened. Jasper began putting on his gloves and Miranda heard the distant sound of his horse being brought around from the stables.

Knowing she only had a moment to spare, she rushed from her hiding space around the corner of the house. "Jasper," she exclaimed, loud enough to get his attention.

He looked over his shoulder and smiled before heading in her direction. Miranda drank in the sight of him. He was properly attired once more. She almost preferred seeing him at his leisure instead of the proper gentleman closing the distance between them.

"Miranda," he said, in that unnerving French accent that caused her blood to race in her veins. He gave her a bow. "Whatever are you doing outside in the cold, *ma chérie?*" He took off his jacket and placed the garment around her shoulders. Such a kindness was going to be her undoing, especially when that lock of unruly hair once more fell rakishly across his brow.

The impulse was too great for her to ignore. Reaching up, she moved the hair from his forehead, and he captured her trembling fingers in his warm hands. Keeping his eyes fixated on her own, he bent forward and kissed the inside of her wrist. Dear Lord... her knees almost buckled when his lips connected with her feverish skin.

"Miranda?"

"Yes?" She continued staring up at his face as if to commit every inch to her memory so she would never forget him. From his green eyes to the dark shadow of stubble roughing his square jaw line, she couldn't take her eyes from him. He was just as fascinating today as last evening and perhaps even more so, in a rugged kind of a way.

"Why are you outside?" he chuckled in amusement as though he had known where her thoughts had gone.

She at last remembered herself and backed up a step. He, in turn, stepped forward and continued to do so until they were out of sight of the front of the manor. It wasn't until she felt the brick wall upon her back that she realized she had nowhere else to turn.

"I had to see you one last time," she murmured in a

breathy whisper. She leaned her head back just so she could once more stare into his eyes.

"I'm certain our paths will cross often, Miranda, at least when I'm on shore," he said, coming so close she could feel the very heat of him radiating from his body. She almost moaned but as she placed her hands upon his muscular chest, instead a gasp escaped her. Her action was meant to halt him from coming any closer but it had the opposite effect when he pulled her into his arms.

"I don't see how that will be possible," she managed to say, while attempting to hold him off. Her pulse quickened and every fiber of her being craved to be held in his arms forever more. She must remember her goal, and Jasper could never fit into her plans.

"Anything is possible, Miranda. We just need to have a little patience. Time will eventually be on our side. I won't always be at sea." He ran a finger down her cheek, causing her to shiver in pleasure.

"It's not about *time*, Jasper, because all the time in the world won't change anything."

He bent forward until his forehead touched her own. "I know we have only just met but, for whatever the reason, I feel drawn to you. Was I mistaken that you feel the same way?"

Her breath caught in her throat to hear his words. "No," she said honestly. "You weren't mistaken."

He cupped her face so she had no choice than to give him her undivided attention. "Then, hopefully, you'll forgive me if I do something I've been craving to do since last night."

She gulped. *Oh no... please don't let him kiss me.* "What's that?" she asked instead, even though she knew what was coming.

"This..."

His lips gently slid across her own as if testing to see if she would accept the gift of his kiss. She should have pulled away but how could she deny what she herself wanted just as badly? She tilted her head to give him full access to her mouth and, when his tongue slipped inside, Miranda was completely lost. Shivers of delight swept across her entire body until she found herself wrapped in Jasper's arms. Her hands made their way up into his hair and her fingers tangled into the soft length. He deepened their kiss without any protest from Miranda until she thought her feet would never again touch the ground.

How long their mouths danced with one another, she could not say. For one brief instant, Miranda never wanted the kiss to end. She never wanted to leave Jasper's arms or his life. But when a soft moan escaped from her lips, the reality of what this man did to her finally penetrated her numb mind. She broke off their kiss and yet their mouths lingered near as their breaths mingled together. She may want him, but he could never offer her the life of her dreams.

"We cannot continue this, Jasper," she quaked, her voice stricken with grief at what she would lose after he was gone. She gulped in deep breaths of air to calm her nerves. He kissed her forehead before stepping backward to a respectable distance. Miranda had never felt colder knowing what was to come.

"Of course. You made me forget myself," Jasper replied as he reached for her hand. He kissed her knuckles before wrapping her hand between the palms of his own. "Your brother-in-law and sister will be coming to see my ship in a few weeks before it sails. Perhaps you can convince them to bring you along so we might see each other again."

A part of her heart soared with joy at his words but she knew that what had just transpired between them was all they would ever have. She might as well get this part of the conversation over with. Wasn't this why she had initially waited for him? She had already let this situation go further than she had planned. It wasn't right for her to lead him to believe that they could be more than just friends.

She gave a heavy sigh before bringing the edges of his coat closer around her neck. She had never felt colder. "I don't see what good can come from us continuing any sort of a relationship, Jasper. If that was your intent, that is." She refused to look into his eyes but he took that choice away from her when his finger tilted up her chin.

"What are you talking about? Of course, I was implying I would like to continue getting to know you better. I thought you wanted the same thing."

She moved around him so she was no longer backed up against the wall. She lifted her chin, determined in her desire to continue her search for a man with a title. She masked her face into an expression that she'd perfected over many years... indifferent, even haughty. Such a look had turned away many a beau who did not fit her criteria of landed and titled gentry.

"Since we are barely acquainted, you don't know what I need, Jasper. I am trying to tell you that I must wed someone with a title." Her voice was quiet but firm. She wasn't sure if she was trying to convince Jasper or herself.

A sound came from his throat that almost sounded like a wounded animal. "You are not a titled lady your-self, Miranda. My birth is perfectly respectable. Not that I was ready to offer marriage, but what difference does it make if your future husband is titled or not?" he asked. His fists clenched at his side. Was he attempting to hold his disappointment in check? Or was it anger?

"It matters to me! You must see that both my brother and sister have titles. It isn't fair that I am denied an honorific," she burst out. "It matters, Jasper." A sob escaped her. Perhaps that was no longer as true as it had been. The thought of not seeing Jasper caused tears to well in her eyes.

"I see," Jasper replied, his eyes flashing fury. He looked her up and down as though finally seeing her for the first time. When his eyes at last met hers, Miranda was heart stricken to no longer see warmth for her reflected there. "I did not take you for one of *those* women who wish for a title no matter the cost. But, as you said, we barely know one another. The mistake was mine to assume otherwise. My moral compass must be off." A smile cracked his lips as he tried to hide the hurt with a joke.

"Jasper, please..." She reached for him but he held up his hand to halt her progress.

"There is no need for further discussion, Miss de Courtenay. I wish you success in finding a gentleman you believe is worthy of you." He gave her a short nod before taking his leave.

Not Miranda... Miss de Courtenay... A formality that sounded out of place considering what had begun between them... and what she had willingly ended. She went to the wall and placed her hand on the corner for support. Jasper mounted his horse and never once looked back as he left Highgrove Manor.

It wasn't until she had run upstairs to her room and flung herself onto her bed for a well-deserved cry that she realized she still had his jacket. She pulled the garment into her chest as if to will Jasper back to her side. And as her tears consumed the better part of the evening, Miranda wondered if, by letting Jasper slip from her grasp, she might have just made the biggest mistake of her entire life.

CHAPTER 6

J asper peered at detailed drawings of *The Legacy*, an exasperated sigh escaping his lips. His ship had been plagued by breakdowns. One repair after another was needed and he began to wonder what he had got into. His plan to leave the London docks by the end of the week now seemed elusive. Not when a rudder chain needed to be mended along with one of the main sails.

"Bloody hell," he swore, before reaching for his cup of coffee. He inhaled the bitter fragrance and took a sip before setting the mug down again. "Is this endeavor doomed?"

Gasparel Beaumonte, his friend since childhood, straightened from his own assessment of the drawings. Jasper had hired him as his First Mate or Chief of their cargo. As another investor, Gasparel had also grown leery of a failed operation.

"It seems to me someone doesn't want us sailing out of London." Gasparel raked a hand through his dark curly hair.

Jasper grimaced. "Hugo Danville?"

"I have yet to find anyone tampering with the ship, *mon ami*," Gasparel said, shrugging. "Once the repairs are made, we can continue to load the goods from your warehouse. It shouldn't take more than a few days."

"Unless something else decides to break down," Jasper muttered. "With all new crew members, it's hard to know who is trustworthy and who isn't."

"I'll keep an extra lookout and maybe we can enlist Dr. Roth to aid us."

"Yes. You can trust the good doctor. He's been a family friend since before I was born," Jasper said going to his desk.

"I almost forgot. There's a gent who's looking for work. He showed up right before I came down to your cabin. Says he was previously Quartermaster in the Navy before he was injured and let go."

"References?"

"In order, along with a remarkable military career." Gasparel handed over the paperwork.

Jasper took several minutes to read the documentation before him. "Impressive. Send him in," Jasper replied. He rolled down his sleeves and donned his jacket.

He didn't have long to wait before a knock sounded upon his door. With a call to enter, a middle-aged sailor took off his cap and stood before him. A patch across his left eye gave him a look of a pirate. Surely the man wasn't retired from the Navy due to an eye injury?

"Captain Rousseau," he said, shaking Jasper's out stretched hand. "I'm George Watson."

"Mr. Watson... A pleasure. I understand from Mr. Beaumonte you are seeking employment on my brig."

"Yes, sir, I am."

"And may I inquire why you are no longer in the Royal Navy?"

The man moved the patch from his eye before putting it back in place. "Lost my sight during a battle that included saving the captain of the ship I was serving on. Instead of being grateful, he deemed me unfit to continue on as Quartermaster. I've been looking for another ship ever since. No one seems to want a one-eyed navigator," he grumbled.

"Well, today is your lucky day, Mr. Watson. You will soon learn I am not like your last captain and I value a good man with an outstanding career. The job is yours if you'd like to sign on."

"Thank you for the chance, Captain. You won't regret bringing me onboard."

The two men left Jasper's cabin before returning up deck. "Mr. Beaumonte," Jasper called out. Gasparel finished his instructions to one of the crew before making his way across the deck.

"Mr. Watson has agreed to sail with us. Show him

about *The Legacy* and see him settled," Jasper ordered, before he noticed his cook coming from below.

Arthur Dennison was a man of many talents, or so Jasper had learned. His brown hair and beard were peppered with gray but his age did not detract from his merry disposition. Jasper had never met someone who so constantly appeared jolly, causing his belly to shake whenever he laughed, which was often.

"Mr. Dennison. I've vacated my cabin to await my guests. If you could see to a light repast in my quarters, I would appreciate it."

"I will endeavor to make your luncheon acceptable for the ladies who will join you," Arthur answered with a wink.

"I'm certain whatever you provide will be adequate."

Arthur laughed. "Adequate? I can do better than adequate!" he announced before taking himself back down below.

Jasper went to the railing and saw his father's carriage pull up to the docks. A footman let down the step and Jasper watched as his parents began making their way carefully over the gangplank. Once his mother was firmly on the deck, she lifted her chin.

"*Maman*," he whispered, after kissing both cheeks. "Welcome aboard *The Legacy*."

"Hello, son," his mother, Sophie, replied. "Your father has done nothing but exclaim his excitement about this boat."

"Ship, my dear," Tavas interjected with a smile.

"Boat... ship... you sail on it so it's all the same to me." Sophie laughed brightly, with a wave of her hand. "Will you show us about, Jasper?"

"In a moment, *Maman*. Lord Nicholas Lacey and his wife will also be joining us. He's investing in our shipping business and should arrive soon."

Sophie shrugged. "I don't understand why you need investors. We have more money already than we know what to do with." Her eyes traveled around the ship.

Tavas put his arm around his wife's shoulders. "Investors means more money coming into the business, my sweet. More business means further expansion."

"I'll trust the details to you, Tavas," she replied. "In either case, your boat... errr... ship looks impressive, son."

He was about to reply when another carriage pulled up alongside the dock. He recognized the Lacey crest on the door. Lord Nicholas alit first, followed by his lady, who waved from the shore. Jasper returned the gesture, but, when the footman held out his hand for another occupant, Jasper's breath caught.

He gulped hard when Miranda left the carriage. She adjusted her shawl around her shoulders before she looked up. A smile hesitated upon her lips, and Jasper swore his heart betrayed him when it flipped end over end inside his chest.

He may have previously invited her to join Nicholas and Grace when they came to visit *The Legacy,* but he never thought Miranda would actually accompany them, given their last conversation. He squared his shoulders, knowing he could do nothing more than welcome Miranda onboard.

His mother came and took his arm. "Who is she?" she asked, a hopeful expression twinkling in her eyes. His mother had been begging him to marry for the past several years and he could imagine her already planning his wedding to this young woman who might have stolen his heart.

"No one... no one at all," Jasper muttered. How would he ever endure the next couple of hours knowing Miranda was on his ship?

CHAPTER 7

Eyes closed, Miranda stood at the bow of *The Legacy* and took a deep breath to calm her shattered nerves. Her pleas to stay at Grace's London town house until they were ready to travel to the coast had fallen on deaf ears. Grace was tired of Miranda's melancholy mood and had told her the outing would do her good. Besides, her sister had insisted, how often did one get a tour of a merchant ship?

How often indeed? Miranda knew next to nothing about ships and generally cared even less about the intricacies of sailing one. It wasn't as though a ship was going to be taking her someplace exciting. When would she ever see Paris? The war with France had lasted most of her life, and she shouldn't be complaining because she was safe and sound on English soil. But somehow, listening to Jasper's deep baritone voice earlier had changed her opinion about being onboard and she had carefully listened to his every word while he took them for a tour of *The Legacy*. She closed her eyes, reliving the day thus far...

The newly constructed cabins were sparse but would provide passengers with the minimum of necessities. Jasper had explained that, although he and his father would take on travelers, cargo remained their main source of income and all extra space was needed to store their goods. This justified the small quarters. Not that it mattered. It wasn't as though Miranda would ever set foot on Jasper's ship again or see him for that matter. So why did her heart continue to ache at the thought of never seeing him again? She shook her head and reasoned that, if she ever traveled by sea, there were plenty of other boats that could take her wherever she needed to go.

As Jasper continued his tour, he had shown them an open doorway to the lower portions of *The Legacy*. He refused, however, to lead them further below, insisting it was no place to take ladies. Instead, he ushered their group to the far end of the passageway. Miranda had been surprised when the door opened and she saw the spaciousness of the room. Obviously, this cabin situated at the stern of the ship was Jasper's. Light from the windows reflected off the water, bringing rays of sunshine into the room. A small desk sat in one corner. Miranda saw another table where parchments of some kind were still open and a quick peak confirmed they were drawings of the ship.

Everyone took a seat at the table set up for dining in the middle of the room and Miranda found herself sitting next to Jasper's mother, who began chatting away as though they were long-lost friends. Miranda recognized her from the ball last month and learned that his French father had married an Englishwoman. From the stolen glances his parents gave one another, Miranda could assume it was a love match.

A light repast had been provided for them but, while tea was being brought into the room, Miranda did everything in her power not to look over at the large bed set into the far wall. It was near impossible, since she was directly across from this particular luxury afforded the captain. Just thinking of Jasper's tall body stretched out between the linen at night caused her heart to hammer away in her chest. This had *not* been a good idea.

His cook had performed a culinary miracle with the food he had provided, and the repast would have been the envy of many of England's best chefs. Small delicate cakes, finger sandwiches, scones and clotted cream had been set out for them to enjoy at their leisure. Soon conversations began to flow and laughter filled the cabin. Miranda couldn't remember the last time she had felt this content.

Their time in the same room seemed to both drag and pass all too quickly. Still... Miranda continued to steal glances at Jasper whenever he appeared preoccupied with other conversations. He looked so handsome in his dark brown jacket and cream-colored trousers. His white linen shirt contrasted with his deeply tanned skin. His cravat was impeccably tied and a golden chain disappeared into a front pocket of his striped waistcoat. She watched when those lean long fingers took hold of the golden fob before opening the watch to take note of the time. As the piece clicked closed and he returned the timepiece to the pocket, their eyes met.

A flicker of something gleamed in those smoldering jade orbs. Appreciation? Caring? Longing? He was hard to read from across the table. Not that she should worry about what he thought of her. After all... she was the one who abruptly ended their short relationship. She took another deep breath. Just thinking of Jasper caused her nerves to become a rattled mess.

"You look as though you belong here, Miranda." That voice broke into her musings, causing a shiver of pleasure to race throughout her body. His tone was gentle. Might Jasper still care for her? *God help me*.

She turned to face him and realized he was closer than she thought. Her breath caught in her throat before she finally answered him. "Do I?" she asked hesitantly, before she shrugged. "I never seem to really fit in anywhere."

"Maybe you're just looking in all the wrong places." His solemn expression seemed genuinely concerned. Miranda's determination to have a titled man as her husband waned in Jasper's presence. It troubled her, and at the same time she felt guilty. Wasn't she being untrue to herself?

"Perhaps," she replied, quietly. She would concede that something inside her was changing. She wasn't sure if she cared for the changes or not, but she couldn't stand to see the hurt she might cause this man once again reflected in his eyes.

A few locks of her hair whisked across her face and Jasper reached out to tuck the length behind her ear. "Miranda—"

"I must apologize if my presence has made you uncomfortable, Jasper. I tried to persuade Grace to pick me up after they were done here," she interrupted. She gestured at the planks beneath her feet. "As you can see, I failed."

"You are more than welcome onboard. But you're not remaining in London?" The ship chose that moment to sway and, before Miranda's stance could falter, Jasper took hold of her elbow to steady her. Her heart betrayed her yet again when he placed her hand into the crook of his arm to offer his support.

"No, I'm afraid not. Nicholas has purchased a cottage on the coast at Cromer in Norfolk. I'm to accompany them and their children while they look the place over and furnish it. It's part of my punishment for past offenses, I suppose. I'd rather not go into the details."

"Spending time with your family hardly seems like punishment, Miranda."

"I'm glad you haven't heard the gossip surrounding me the past few years. Elsewise, you'd be like the rest of the *ton* and stay away from me at all costs. I'm only really accepted among them because of Grace and Adrian."

He pulled her to face him and lifted her chin. "We may not have known one another for long, but you must know I'm not cut from the same mold as most of society. I've lived by my own rules, and, while I try to remain the gentleman my parents raised me to be, I don't mind taking a risk now and then."

"Like at the ball?" she asked, trying to keep her nerves calm.

"Yes. I thought you also didn't mind occasionally dismissing the convention of men and women of their ilk since you decided to dance with me."

She thought of how a foolish bet with Grace had almost been the ruin of her reputation at Hollystone Hall. A laugh escaped her. "If you only knew..."

"Perhaps one day you shall confide in me. I promise to keep your secrets." His grin was completely wicked, and another piece of her heart melted.

"I just may hold you to your vow, Jasper," she teased, her eyes twinkling in merriment while they jested with one another.

They began to stroll along the deck. Jasper set a leisurely pace as if he, too, didn't wish for this moment to end. It was almost as if their conversation at Highgrove Manor never occurred.

"Will you return for the rest of the Season?" he inquired, stopping at the rail opposite where she would leave the ship. Had he planned that they were conveniently hidden from Grace and his parents behind some large cargo roped off and wrapped in tarp?

She tried to still her erratic heart and failed. "My plans are to travel south to visit with my friend Lady Jane Wallace. She and her husband have recently moved to Southwold. She asked if I could come and stay with her during her confinement." A blush heated her face at the turn their conversation had taken. "Good heavens. You must forgive me. I'm such a chatterbox and shouldn't be discussing such matters with a gentleman."

His chuckle told Miranda much. She may have angered him at their last meeting, but there was still something obviously drawing them together with invisible ties. The pull that connected them was hard to ignore and warred inside of her heart. "No need to apologize, Miranda. Believe me I've heard far worse living on board a ship."

He ran a finger down her cheek and she did everything in her power not to lean into his hand. "But certainly, never from a lady, I hope." She gazed up into his eyes and once more realized her mistake when those green orbs twinkled in merriment.

"Only from you, and I still hold you in the highest esteem no matter how much I think your aspiration for a title is misguided."

She wanted to be insulted by his words, but it was

hard to muster up any indignation when he pulled her closer, after looking around to ensure they were still alone. "I thought you said your moral compass was broken where I was concerned," she murmured, caressing the edges of his jacket.

"Perhaps it was only a little misguided. I can't help but still feel we belong together." His roguish grin and chuckle were almost her undoing but it was nothing compared to when he quickly leaned down and stole a brief kiss.

"I should go," she whispered, while her lips tingled from the contact of his mouth on hers. She needed to leave him before she completely lost her heart to this man. He would ruin all her plans for a different life.

"I wish you didn't have to," he said, his husky tone once again turning her insides to mush. He leaned forward and brushed his lips against her forehead and she sighed. How she wished he could be more than a mere captain of a ship.

"I wish you safe travels on your coming journey," she whispered, before pulling out of his arms. She took several steps backward and memorized his features. "Farewell, Jasper."

Turning away from him, she began to distance herself from the man who had somehow stolen her heart. But her footsteps faltered when he called out to her again.

"Every time you walk away, you're going to take a piece of my heart."

A groan escaped her, because his words mirrored her own thoughts. She tried not to cry when she turned toward him one last time. "I'm certain your manly pride will somehow survive, Captain," she teased instead. She watched his smile broaden before he laughed.

Dipping into a curtsey, she made a hasty retreat before she completely succumbed to Jasper's charms. It wouldn't take much effort on his part to make her change her mind about whom she should marry.

Hugo Danville stood in the shadows of a building on the wharf, pulling several coins from a pouch inside his jacket. He handed them to the seaman standing before him.

"You've done well so far. Be sure to continue to wreak havoc on *The Legacy* and I'll double your pay. Do not fail me." Hugo waved the man off. Their business was concluded.

"Ye can count on me, Gov'nr," the seaman replied before slipping away into the crowded docks.

Hugo pushed off the brick building and began strolling down the docks heading toward the inn he had been staying at. There was a woman leaving *The Legacy*. Rousseau came to the railing and watched her depart. It was obvious the captain must have feelings for the young woman.

Another plan began forming in Hugo's mind, and he

chuckled at his own cleverness. As he watched the woman's carriage depart, he hired a hack and told the driver to follow them. He rubbed his hands in glee just thinking of another way to thwart the Rousseaus.

Jasper's heart sank as he watched the lady disappear into the Lacey carriage and vanish away from the crowded wharf. What else could he have done other than to let her go? Again! He certainly couldn't proclaim his intentions, nor could he announce how he truly had begun to care for her. He wasn't ready to give Miranda the leverage of knowing he had so readily fallen for her. Not when she was determined to fulfill some childish dream of wedding a peer.

He supposed he shouldn't have been surprised the lady was after a title. So many young ladies were. But still... the memory of her standing at the bow of his ship with the long ends of her shawl billowing behind her in the breeze was one he wasn't likely to forget anytime soon. The beautiful image of her had engraved itself into his very soul. He had been truthful when he told her she seemed to belong on his ship. If only...

Jasper muttered a curse and returned to what mattered for the time being. He had a voyage to worry about, and he would do his best to forget the fair Miranda. There was no sense in wondering if this budding infatuation with the young lady might bear fruit. She had told him what she wanted in life and unfortunately that didn't include a mere captain of a ship. Maybe he should take up a mistress, but he dispelled the idea as soon as it entered his head. The thought might once have been appealing, but the only woman he wanted in his bed was the one who had just left him.

CHAPTER 8

Miranda stepped into the coaching inn in Norwich and promptly bumped into a gentleman who was leaving. Strong arms wound around her waist to keep her from falling while her hands stretched across a firmly muscled chest. A gasp escaped her when she looked up into his dark brown eyes while a slight grin swept across his mouth. She blinked several times as his black hair blew in the breeze from the entryway. Once she was again on firm ground, he released her.

"My sincere apologies, Lady..." he inquired, giving her a courtly bow that appeared as though it should be given in a ballroom instead of an inn. He waved his arm to allow her entrance.

"Miss de Courtenay," she replied without thinking, leading the way into the establishment with her maid Elsie directly behind her. Elsie was actually Grace's maid but her sister had allowed Miranda to travel with her when Grace felt indisposed and unfit to travel farther than their newly acquired cottage. Her sister's illness must surely have rattled Grace's wits, because she exclaimed Miranda could hardly get into trouble in one day's time. Miranda kept silent, happy for the freedom to continue on her way to Lady Jane's house in Southwold.

The morning was nearly gone and Miranda's only thought was to get back on the road once the coach changed horses. If she was lucky, they could make it to her friend's before nightfall, and she could attend Sunday services in the morning, if Jane felt up to the excursion. A brief gaze out the window at the stormy skies allowed a moment of worry to crease her brow. The last thing she needed was another delay in reaching her destination. It had been raining all morning.

Miranda found an unoccupied table and, after a pot of hot tea and two cups were set before her, she began to pour. She had just handed one of the cups to Elsie when a tall form blocked her view of the window. The gentleman took hold of the empty chair next to Miranda, the sound of wood scrapping across the floor causing Miranda to pause what she was doing. The man had the gall to sit. Apparently, when she bumped into him, he thought this was some sort of an invitation. Her brow rose at his forwardness.

"I didn't have the chance to introduce myself," he said flashing a smile that probably had most women swooning. But she had never been drawn to men with dark hair, and her memories of Jasper quickly flitted across her mind. Perhaps she should widen her scope of the men who usually appealed to her. "I am Hugo Danville. My father, Lord Lansbury, and I are to visit our ship the *Acacia* on business. She is docked in Yarmouth. What brings you to town?"

Miranda set down the teapot, intrigued that a titled gentleman had practically fallen right into her lap, although she was surprised she had not heard of his father. She thought she was familiar with all the peers of England. Perhaps it was a Scottish or Irish title.

The gentleman's tone implied she should be impressed with his announcement he was nobility. She opened and closed her mouth several times trying to form a reply but she had no idea who this man was. She certainly wasn't about to divulge her travel plans.

"Lord Danville," she murmured politely, before placing her hands in her lap. She stole a glance at Elsie who looked uneasy. "My business is my own, sir." She tossed him a look that had left more than one beau running for the door, but such was not the case with the man before her. His grin only widened and she took a sip of her tea to distract herself from this all too handsome rogue. She had the distinct feeling in her bones this man was used to getting his way She wasn't familiar with the title 'Lansbury', but he must be an earl or a marquess, for she had called his son 'Lord', and he had not corrected her.

"Perhaps I could procure a private room so we might enjoy a meal together?" he proposed raising his hand to call over the innkeeper.

She almost spewed her tea across the table. "I should think not!" she managed to squeak out, before setting down her cup. "I do not know who you are, Lord Danville, but I am not accustomed to talking with nor taking refreshments with unknown men."

He leaned back into his chair, his hands forming a steeple when he rested his elbows on the arms of his seat. His fingers went to his lips as he contemplated her before he relaxed.

"I meant no disrespect, Miss de Courtenay. You intrigue me and I only wished to get to know you better." He reached over and grabbed her hand so fast Miranda had no time to react. He quickly kissed the air between his lips and her knuckles, and she was surprised when a sudden blush rushed across her cheeks.

She pulled her hand away and was at a loss for words. This man presumed too much on a chance encounter with an unknown lady. "A gentleman would know the proper way for an introduction to occur, sir."

"Then point me in the direction of your parents so I might plead my cause," he said looking about the room, but Miranda had the notion he already knew she traveled alone.

"I'm afraid that's impossible," she stated, before taking another sip of her tea. She tried not to think of her parents and how they had been gone from this world for many years.

"You look sad and that was not my intention," he declared while worry and concern etched its way across his features. "I pray your parents have not..."

"They are..." Miranda interrupted. "Gone several years now."

"My condolences on your loss, my lady," he said, patting her hand before taking the liberty of pouring more tea into her cup. "I wouldn't have brought up memories of your loved ones had I only known."

"Thank you, Lord Danville," Miranda replied, finally relaxing in his company. He appeared so sincere when he offered her an encouraging smile that she completely overlooked the fact he had introduced himself. She tried not to over think why she wasn't uneasy with the lack of a formal introduction with Lord Danville. Was it only because she assumed he was nobility? This had certainly been her main concern with Jasper when they first met.

"I only wish I had more time to linger in your company. Alas, I am on my way to our ship at Yarmouth and can delay my business no longer. Is there a relative near where I can leave my card and perhaps call upon you at a later time?"

Miranda hesitated in giving out information on where she was headed. Instead, she gave him a bright smile. After all... he was titled and he might be just what she needed to get Jasper out of her mind. "My brother-in-law Lord Nicholas Lacey and my sister are residing in Cromer. You may leave your card there if you happen to travel in that direction."

"I shall indeed make the effort to get myself to Cromer then," he beamed with another bright smile. "I will look forward to when our paths cross again, Miss de Courtenay."

"As will I, Lord Danville," she answered with a nod of her head.

"Ladies..." he said, giving Elsie a wink that caused her maid to gasp. Lord Danville stood but, before he took his leave, he bent down to whisper in Miranda's ear. "I look forward to seeing you again, Miss de Courtenay. I guarantee you shall enjoy *my* company far above anyone else you might meet." He gave a short bow and left the inn.

Elsie set her cup down. "What a horrible man!"

"Nonsense, Elsie. He was utterly delightful, although I must admit I was at first leery when he just assumed he had our permission to join us without asking first."

"You would think that a gentleman would have better manners."

Miranda's gave a light laugh. "Not everyone plays by the rules of polite society, Elsie, and Lord Danville seems to go after what he wants." Miranda tried not to think about why the son of a marquess would be interested in a woman with no title. But no matter... if Lord Danville was interested in her, then perhaps she just might find herself wed to a title after all. Miranda also knew a thing or two about going after what a person wanted. She had been trying to do the exact same thing for more years than she could count!

When the coachman entered the inn to announce they were ready to travel again, Miranda was more than relieved to leave Norwich behind. Luckily, Grace and Nicholas had hired a coach, so Miranda and Elsie had the conveyance to themselves.

But as they continued traveling overland beyond Norwich, she grew more and more concerned. The skies darkened until day turned almost to night. Larger raindrops began pelting the windows followed by huge balls of hail. Not long afterwards the coach came to a halt and the driver opened the hatch to call down they were going to have to detour from the main highway and take a less traveled route out to the coast road due to flooding on the main road.

The weather continued to get worse, and the glimpses of the muddy mess that had once been a road confirmed her gravest fears as the coachman made one turn after another.

She barely made out a sign of a village named Fenwick on Sea before the coach hit a large rut causing the coach to tilt. She let out a scream when she was bounced from her seat. The coach began to list. Miranda strained her ears over the storm to hear the coachman yelling at the team of horses when he yanked on the reins bringing them to another halt. Miranda righted herself and returned to the seat but held onto the ledge of the window. Elsie looked just as terrified as they waited with bated breath for the entire conveyance to topple over at any second.

The door to the coach was yanked open and a torrential downpour began flooding into the interior. Two wet oiled coats were handed over to the women while the coachman quickly explained their predicament.

"We broke an axle, Miss. Luckily we're only a short distance from the Queens Barque. Tommy an' I will help ye and yer maid get to the inn an' we'll come back fer yer luggage an' the 'orses."

Thankful for the walking boots she had on, Miranda welcomed assistance to leave the coach, especially given the slippery mud beneath her. She was glad the coachman knew where they were going, because, with the hood of the oiled coat over her head, Miranda could hardly make out anything as the rain continued to beat down on her.

They finally reached the inn and Miranda saw it was, at core, an old Tudor style building with several wings that looked to have been built in every century since. When they entered, the sounds of conversations seemed deafening, as though all of the countryside were currently residing inside. A voice rang out above the sound of others.

"We have another guest," the man's voice boomed as he flung a bar towel over his shoulder.

A matronly woman began making her way to

Miranda, who took off the oiled coat and handed it to the coachman. He hurried back toward the door. As he opened it, an oversized dog with big floppy ears came bounding into the entryway. He began shaking the water from his coat.

The dog cocked his head as if assessing Miranda while she stared into his searching eyes. The dog's mouth hung open and he began to drool, making Miranda wonder if she was his next meal. The animal's head reached her waist, and Miranda began to shake with fear. She stepped back from the dog, which appeared as if it was a mix of mastiff and heaven only knew what. The dog came to sit before her, lifted up a paw apparently so she could shake it and then his plumed tail began to wag.

"Off with you now, Hector," the woman scolded the dog. "No worries, my lady. He's friendly enough but must have escaped the coach house. Will you be needing a room for the night?"

"Yes, if you have something available," Miranda replied, trembling from the cold. "I'm thankful to be out of the storm."

"Oh, you poor sweet lamb," the woman cooed. "I'm Mrs. Brewster. My husband and I run the Queen's Barque. Let's get you up to a room."

"I am most grateful, Mrs. Brewster," Miranda replied.

"We're nigh full up. We still have a vacant room but

your maid will need to bed down with the other servants. I hope that won't inconvenience you much."

Miranda's gaze swept the crowded bar where every table was filled. "I'm sure we can make do, Mrs. Brewster. If you could perhaps have a bath sent up, that would be lovely."

"Of course," Mrs. Brewster said before waving towards a young woman. "This is my daughter, Charlotte. I know you're busy, dear, but have one of the lads fetch the tub and have hot water sent up to room number three for Lady..."

"Miss de Courtenay," Miranda replied, once again glum over her lack of a title.

"I'll take care of it, mum," Charlotte replied, before scurrying off to do her mother's bidding.

"This way, Miss de Courtenay," Mrs. Brewster said, before heading toward a set of stairs along the far wall of the room.

Miranda followed behind Mrs. Brewster while the woman chatted on about what in the village might be of interest once the weather cleared, including a Norman church. They hadn't gone far down the hallway before Miranda was shown to a room with modest furnishings. This inn had certainly seen better times but she would in no way complain about the accommodations. She was lucky to have a bed to sleep in tonight, and at least she was having an adventure.

Before long, a tub of hot water was set before the fire in the hearth, with a small meal left within reach of the bather. When the luggage arrived, Elsie left out a nightgown for Miranda to put on once she was finished with her bath. Miranda sunk into the calming hot water and sighed in relief as the bath began to work its magic. She could only wonder what tomorrow would bring. Until the coach was repaired, she would be stranded at the Queen's Barque.

Hugo could not believe his luck! Of all the places Miss de Courtenay could have found herself, it would be the place Hugo was doing a bit of business.

He returned his attention to the men at his table and began discussing the contraband he had for sale. He had been cursing the need to travel in this weather, but it was becoming a most profitable and pleasant excursion after all!

CHAPTER 9

Aboard *The Legacy*, Friday morning gave way to early afternoon with the clouds thickening. Jasper checked the barometer and wasn't pleased with what he saw. "I don't like the look of this," he complained bitterly, before raising his eyes to the thunderous clouds above. "I've got to be the biggest idiot in all of England *and* France to be sailing out into weather like this."

"What option do we have?" Gasparel asked, holding the hood of his oiled coat while the wind tried to wretch it from his hand. "We couldn't sail in the storm earlier this week. If you don't think this is going to blow over, we could delay another day."

Jasper swore. "And miss the delivery date of our cargo? That's really not an option."

"Then we must get underway before the tide is no

longer in our favor. Surely we can make it across the Channel without further incident?"

"One can only hope." Jasper scanned the dock and finally saw the carriage he had been waiting for. "Looks like the last of our passengers decided to show up. I'd best go greet them. As soon as they're onboard, along with their luggage, take us out while I show them to their cabins."

"Aye, Captain," his first mate exclaimed, before standing next to the wheel.

Jasper descended from the taffrail and met Lord Hythe at the railing. "Welcome aboard *The Legacy*, my lord."

Hythe extended his hand and the two men shook. "Sorry for the delay, Captain Rousseau, but my sister's maid is not too keen on traveling."

"It happens to the best of us," Jasper replied politely. He glanced at the girl, who looked positively green, and they hadn't even left the dock yet.

"Fliss, may I present our captain, Captain Jasper Rousseau. Captain, my sister, Lady Felicity Belvoir, and her maid Miss Theodosia Conroy," Hythe continued. Jasper contained his astonishment at being introduced to a servant. He'd heard the Belvoir family called progressive in their thinking, and apparently it was true.

Jasper gave a short nod. "A pleasure, ladies, but let's get you out of the rain and into your cabins. You'll at least be warm and out of the elements."

Taking them below, he first showed Hythe to his

cabin before opening the door next to his wide enough for the ladies to enter. Their luggage followed right behind them and Miss Conroy all but fell into a nearby chair.

"We may encounter rough water due to the storm," Jasper explained, trying not to alarm the women but it was best they were prepared. "Please stay inside your cabin."

"We'll be sure to do so," Lady Felicity responded, her eyes twinkling. "We'd hate to be a distraction."

He gave them a brief nod before heading down the passageway. Another ladder took him to the galley, where he braced himself on the door frame while addressing his cook. "Mr. Dennison, have a pot of hot tea sent to cabin four for the two women on board. Afterward, it's light rations until we're out of the storm. No sense on a fire breaking out during inclement weather."

A snarky laugh left his cook. "This isn't my first trip to sea, captain. I've got my galley handled. You take care of sailing this ship," he quipped before pointing toward a kettle already heating on the stove.

Knowing he'd done the best he could for the two ladies on board until the storm was over, he returned topside and took a firm grip upon the wheel. If it wasn't for the rain pounding upon his body, he would have enjoyed the moment of getting underway. The recent pitfalls that had befallen his ship were still a mystery; they had yet to figure out exactly who was deliberately causing one thing after another to fail. Sails didn't just get slashed; rudder chains didn't break as though someone had cut through them.

Hugo Danville continued to be in the forefront of his mind. It wouldn't be the first time his nemesis had tried to ruin his business, nor did Jasper feel it would be the last. But there was no longer any time to ponder what Danville planned next. If he had someone in his employ on *The Legacy*, the man would be found out eventually.

Once they left the Thames, Jasper's muscles strained while keeping his ship on course in the open Channel. Roaring winds whipped at the sails as the storm gained momentum coming down from the North. The barometer had not lied.

They fought the wind all that night and on into the next day as the storm built. Approaching the coast—either the port at Ostend that was their destination or any other port that might grant them haven—was too dangerous in these seas and winds. But Jasper did his best to hold position so that he could take advantage of the first break in the weather to deliver his passengers and his cargo to their destination.

By early Sunday morning, the worst was over, though the rain still drummed on the deck and the small bits of canvas he sported to keep *The Legacy* turned into the wind. By noon, he could begin his run to the coast of Europe—further off than it should be if that was England he saw in the far distance between squalls.

As prepared as he was to handle his ship, he wasn't ready when he heard a loud crack. His eyes turned upward to the forward mast and widened when one of the cross timbers snapped. As the lines and rigging also began to give way, the falling spar ripped open another sail in its descent to deck.

He barely heard the cry ring out when one of his crew got caught in the falling wreckage. Jasper called out orders to rescue him from the debris.

"Mr. Watson," he yelled out to his Quartermaster over the storm. "We make for the nearest port we can find on the English coast. Take the wheel while I head to my cabin briefly to look at my charts."

Once inside his cabin, Jasper quickly scanned the chart laid open before him. Running his finger over the parchment, he assessed any ports to the north. If he was right about how far north they'd drifted with the storm, Yarmouth was the closest port where *The Legacy* could make repairs once it was berthed. He'd head in that direction.

Back on deck, Jasper found out his sailor had sustained several injuries. Other men were in the rigging putting up the sails that were necessary to get them to their new destination. Jasper took the wheel. The ship rocked back and forth with the heavy waves of the channel and Jasper prayed his passengers were weathering the storm.

But it wasn't until he could barely make out the coast that the unthinkable happened... again. The rudder cable snapped. He could only watch in horror as the wind blew *The Legacy* off course and it began to drift further south than Jasper's intended destination. He could hardly make out the shore.

Jasper began to call out orders for jury-rigging a sea anchor, when a sudden side draft caught the ship and the entrance of a river or inlet began to rush upon them at alarming speed. He barely had time to yell for everyone to take hold when the ship slammed into a rocky shoal. *The Legacy* teetered on an angle and Jasper held his breath when it settled.

Chaos erupted among the crew until Jasper took control again, bellowing orders above the wind to check the passengers, hull and cargo. He then began ordering the first of several cables to be strung from the ship to the shore to secure it and its cargo. They'd next need to see to getting the passengers to safety.

Men began readying the skiff to be lowered to the water below. Those who had been injured would be removed first, including Dr. Roth who had banged his head, although he insisted he could still attend the others. Jasper sent Gasparel to inform the passengers to be ready when he returned for them to disembark.

Mr. Watson came up to the taffrail holding a sailor's arm in his meaty fist. "We found our culprit, Captain. Caught him red handed trying to cut through the spare rudder cables on deck."

"Well done, Mr. Watson, but we have no time to question him further at the moment. The passenger's safety and undamaged cargo are our priority. Take him down below to the hold and lock him in a cell," Jasper said, glaring at the man who had caused so much lost time and damage to his ship. "We'll deal with him once the storm is over."

"What if the cells are flooded with water," George asked.

"I'm sure you'll think of something so he is... detained." Jasper waved the men off but remained satisfied he'd have his answers soon as to whom the man worked for.

Jasper went to help with his injured crewmen, praying there were accommodations of some kind in the local village and rooms for a makeshift hospital.

CHAPTER 10

M iranda entered the entrance hall and saw a familiar face. She made her way over to the lady to extend a greeting.

"Miss Meadows, how lovely to see you here among so many strangers," Miranda said cheerfully.

"Miss de Courtenay! What a pleasant and unexpected surprise," the lady replied, before leaning forward and lowering her voice. "Actually, I've recently wed. I'm Lady Stanton now."

"Congratulations on your marriage, my lady," she replied, although inwardly she cringed at the thought of another commoner snagging a title while she remained unattached.

"Thank you. You must be stranded here like the rest of us. Tragedy already struck yesterday when one of the castaways from a shipwreck died in the high tide."

"How horrible!" Miranda said. She scanned the room looking for a vacant table.

"Were you about to take tea?"

"I was planning to. I see a woman alone at a table. Perhaps she will allow us to sit with her," Miranda said, before she began heading in that direction.

"Excuse me, miss. Do you mind if we join you?" Miranda asked, hoping the woman would allow them to sit.

The lady looked up from the book she was reading before her gaze around the room showed all the other occupied tables.

"By all means," she said with a smile, gesturing to the empty chairs.

"Thank you, so very much. I am Miss de Courtenay, but please call me Miranda," she stated before taking a seat. "This is Lady Stanton."

"Please call me Josephine," Lady Stanton replied.

"Miss Eugenia Fynlock." The lady extended her hand in greeting to each of the women.

A serving girl came and took their orders before scurrying off to the kitchen.

Miranda pulled her shawl closer around her shoulders. "We're old acquaintances but we accidentally just met in the entrance hall and decided to dine together. The inn is so crowded. You were very kind to share your table with us."

Miss Fynlock nodded, and the two other women continued their conversations while Miranda began wondering how long she might be stuck here in Fenwick on Sea. She would much rather be sitting in Jane's parlor than in this rundown inn swarming with all of humanity.

But she would rise above her situation and make the most of it, even though she was bored to tears. After all, she couldn't magically fix the coach or drain the floods so she could be on her way, nor could she change the weather. She swore last night she had been waiting for the roof above her head to collapse, given the deluge of rain that had pounded on the window.

One of the ladies interrupted the musings about yesterday's fiasco.

"And I heard that a reporter from that nasty *Teatime Tattler* has taken up residence inside this very inn," Josephine said.

Good heavens... not a reporter from the Tattler, Miranda thought, worrying she'd be the subject of another scandalous article about her. She scanned the room and was surprised to see none other than Lord Danville sitting in a darkened booth with several men. Whatever was he doing here? Despite the weather outside, things were indeed looking a bit brighter with his presence.

"Best be careful of your reputation, ladies," Miranda warned as she came back from thoughts of the handsome man she met just yesterday. "You don't want to end up as the latest tittle-tattle for all of Society to learn about."

The maid returned with a pot of tea and Miranda took the initiative to pour for her newfound friends.

"The information about the reporter is troubling. Perhaps what is needed is a plan to get out of this inn and away from prying eyes and ears," Eugenia suggested.

"Interesting," Josephine remarked, before taking a sip of her tea.

"I'd love to escape this inn for a time," Miranda exclaimed, wondering if Lord Danville might accompany her on the outing. "But the weather is hardly conducive to excursions."

"I agree," Eugenia said. "What if we plan to take an outing on the first good day? The rain is already subsiding. With luck we might go as early as tomorrow afternoon."

"But where?" Josephine queried.

"I was told by Mrs. Brewster when I arrived that the village church is a fine example of Norman architecture and was visited by Queen Elizabeth," Miranda suggested, repeating the information the innkeeper's wife had relayed to her. "She informed me the stained-glass window in the church is supposedly a gift from that noble monarch."

"That's an excellent idea." Eugenia smiled before reaching for her teacup. "My traveling companion is acquainted with Mr. Somerville, the vicar. She assisted him with aiding the injured from this storm. She could ask him if he would guide us through the church."

"Would your friend be Miss Walford?" Josephine asked.

Eugenia nodded. "She is."

"I met her when she was helping the vicar. She has a very tender heart."

"Thank you. I agree. Shall I ask her to speak with Mr. Somerville? I'm sure she'll want to get out of the inn as much as any of us."

"That would be wonderful, Eugenia," Miranda replied while she blushed, thinking of asking Lord Danville to join her.

"Then we are in accord. I will send notes to you both via Mrs. Brewster when I know the details of our visit to the church." Eugenia began eating their lunch when it arrived.

Miranda was busy thinking of ways to arrange an outing with Lord Danville when she heard a distant bell sounding out an alarm. She didn't give it much thought since she was unfamiliar with the workings of this seaside village. But when a man came rushing into the room drenched from the rain, all that changed.

"Been another wreck..." he started to say, while gasping for breath as if he'd run the entire coast. "This time it's on the other side of the inlet and blocking the fishing harbor. Stuck on the rocky shoal, it is. They've got casualties!"

Men and some women rose from their tables to go to the ship's aide. Miranda returned to the remainder of her tea until a conversation stood out from the group about to leave.

"What's the name of the ship?" someone asked the man, who sat with a cup of hot coffee to warm his hands.

"*The Legacy*," he replied before taking a gulp of his brew. "Never been here before and it's not going anywhere for a spell till repairs are done.

When Miranda heard the wreck was Jasper's ship, she shot to her feet so quickly she nearly toppled her chair. "Good heavens... Jasper!"

She turned to flee the inn when her arm was taken by none other than Lord Danville.

"Why, Miss de Courtenay!" he exclaimed, his eyes twinkling in delight. "Wherever are you off to in such a hurry?"

While on any other occasion she would have been more than thrilled this handsome man was having a conversation with her, now was not the time for an idle chit chat.

"I must apologize, Lord Danville, but you will have to excuse me." She wrenched her arm from his grasp and gave him no further thought.

Running through the entrance hall, she grabbed an old oiled great coat hanging on a peg and thrust her arms through the sleeves. The hood was barely over her head before she was out the door and running to catch up with those who were heading toward the wreck to help.

Her feet sunk in the wet sand of the dunes but this was no time to be worried about her shoes. Jasper might be in danger! She trudged ever onward until she reached the edge of the harbor. A low skiff was bouncing over the rough waves while men with bulging muscles pulled it across the water by a heavy cable. It had just reached the shore when Miranda came up to the boat as it hit the shingle at the water's edge. Two women and a man looked grateful to be on solid ground.

She went to help the women from the small boat and recognized three of the occupants immediately; an earl and his sister, along with *The Legacy's* surgeon, Dr. Roth. "My word, Lady Felicity!" Miranda commented over the howling wind.

Before the lady could respond, her brother came to help his sister's maid. "Miss de Courtenay... we must get Miss Conroy settled. Please follow us," Hythe ordered, putting his arm around the maid's waist to support her. "This is no place for a young lady to be out in such elements!"

"Yes, of course," she answered, even though she stood there in indecision. She should go back to the safety of the inn but, when she saw Jasper's ship at a ghastly angle, her only thought was to see firsthand that he was unharmed.

Another man came to lift the maid in his arms, and Hythe and his sister followed him along the shore. Miranda went up to the men who were ready to once more pull the skiff back over to *The Legacy*. "Take me over," she ordered the men before jumping into the small boat.

"But miss..." one of the men began in protest.

"Take me over now or I'll find a way to get there myself!"

She held onto the edge of the boat and, after a brief argument, one jumped in to ensure she made it over the rough water. She began to doubt the wisdom of her actions as the waves splashed over the sides and rocked the tiny vessel as though the sea would like nothing more than to have it sink to the bottom of the harbor. If she was wet when she first ran out into the storm, it was nothing compared to how she was now as the bottom of the skiff filled with water. Her shoes and stockings were drenched while her petticoat clung to her body like a second skin. But she held on for dear life and before long she was at the side of the ship. Looking up at the ladder she would now have to traverse in order to obtain her goal, she shook any doubts from her head and began to climb.

Hand over hand she made her way up until strong hands reached to pull her over the rail to safety. When her feet hit the slippery deck, she fell into Jasper's arms.

"What the bloody hell are you doing here, Miranda?" he yelled before pulling her away from the railing.

"What does it look like? I'm here to make sure you are safe." She held her chin up and the wind took the hood from her head while rain soaked her hair. His eyes blazed in anger and a curse left his lips.

"Mr. Beaumonte," Jasper called out and the man came running over.

"Aye, Captain?"

"See that the next set of passengers disembark while I take care of this insolent young miss. She can wait for the next boat, since we have those who are injured and need immediate medical attention once on shore."

Jasper didn't wait for an answer. Instead, he pulled Miranda down below until they reached his cabin. Flinging open the door, he pushed her inside and the door slammed shut behind them. Miranda unsteadily made her way over to the stern window, distancing herself from the angry man before her. The ghastly angle of the ship made her wonder once more if she had made a mistake. Would it topple over at any moment? She stood shivering now that she was no longer outside but it could also be from being alone... with Jasper... in his cabin.

But the look he gave her had nothing to do with passion even as her eyes roamed over every inch of his body. He appeared to be fine... at least physically.

His mouth was set in a harsh frown when he crossed the room to her. Taking hold of her arms, he shook her as though this would knock some sense into her. "I don't have time to deal with you. How stupid to be out here in the middle of a storm. Or didn't you think about your own damn safety when you decided on your course of action?" he growled out in frustration.

"I needed to make sure you were safe!" she cried out,

thankful he appeared as well as could be expected under the circumstances.

"Why? You made it clear at Highgrove Manor we weren't suited and you were only after some lofty title and the life such a *bagatelle* would give you. Why does it matter to you how I fared?" His raised voice was loud enough to be heard over the wind and waves, probably all the way to the shore on the other side of the inlet. She watched him take in slow deep breaths as though to calm his growing anger.

"Because I still care," she admitted, even while her eyes widened at her admission. Considering she had leapt into a bobbing boat in the middle of a storm just to check on his safety, she should have realized just how much Jasper meant to her. But she hadn't thought of how those actions would look to the outside world. She did that now. She gulped... hard. "I didn't think..."

"No, you didn't," he said. But his anger faded from his eyes as he took time to examine her. "Good Lord, you're soaked to the bone. You'll be sick before nightfall if you stay in those wet clothes."

The angle of the cabin deck obviously didn't hinder Jasper when he easily went over to the trunk at the foot of his bed and pulled out one of his linen shirts. He tossed it on the bed. Before she knew what he was planning, he returned to her side and ripped the oiled great coat from her body, tossing it to the floor. Turning her around, he started to undo the tiny buttons of her gown.

"Jasper," she said trying to distance herself from him without any success, "Stop it this instant."

"Stop struggling!" he warned. "I have no intention of harming you." He pulled her back against his chest. His hands settled upon her shoulders as though to offer some form of comfort before he continued to unbutton her sodden gown.

"Whatever are you doing?"

"Obviously assisting you out of your clothing, my dear. But don't worry... your virtue shall remain intact. As I said, I don't have time to worry over you right now. Not when my passengers and cargo are my priority. Now hold still."

Mortified when her gown was thrown over her head and she stood before him in only her corset, chemise, and stockings, she hid her face in her hands, barely able to understand how she put herself into such a circumstance.

"What will people think if they find out I'm here?" she whispered in embarrassment and horror. She would in no way be able to salvage her reputation after this.

"You should have thought of *that* before you had someone row you out to my ship, *ma chérie*," Jasper murmured before he put a blanket over her shoulders.

The endearment as it left his lips surprised her and, when she looked up into his face, she saw a hint of appreciation in the small smile he gave her. He appeared no longer angry with her, and Miranda wasn't sure if she should be relieved or concerned she was alone with him.

"Put on my shirt and crawl into bed. You'll at least be warm there. I'll come back as soon as I'm able and will take you back to shore myself."

Miranda stood where she was as if frozen while he made his way to the door. "Jasper... wait." She ran across the room and flung herself into his arms and he captured her against his chest. "I'm so thankful you weren't injured during the wreck."

He held her firmly with one arm and her heart fluttered inside her chest when her eyes met his. Something shifted inside her and Miranda knew she would never be the same again. She crushed her lips against his own in a searing kiss that was far shorter than she would have liked.

"What was that for, *ma petite*?" he asked, his smirk cocky.

"It was in case I don't get the chance to kiss you later," she answered honestly, before heat rushed to her cheeks.

A chuckle escaped him before he quickly kissed her again. He set her down and gave her a slight push away from him. "Get into bed, Miranda."

He left her. It was probably for the best. As she pulled his shirt over her own body and crawled between the sheets of his bed, she began to wonder exactly what she had landed herself in. She may have just sealed her own fate with Jasper.

Hugo checked his watch for what seemed like the hundredth time. When Miranda didn't return with the rest of the people pouring into the inn who needed medical attention, he became more than annoyed. He would need to find a way to get the lovely young lady to himself if only to further irritate Rousseau. He was certain he'd come up with some idea before he concluded his business in Fenwick on Sea.

CHAPTER 11

S everal hours later, Jasper was finally able to deal with the lady who awaited him in his cabin. He had decided to keep her safe in his cabin until the rest of the passengers and cargo had been seen to. It was probably a mistake to add onto hers—the one that brought her here to *The Legacy* in the first place.

He hesitated briefly with his fingertips on the handle before he discreetly knocked upon his own damn door. When he heard the call to enter, he went inside, not knowing what to expect from the beautiful but unpredictable Miranda. She spouted about wanting a husband with a title, but her actions today said otherwise. She must know her reputation would be in ruins if others learned she was aboard his ship and unchaperoned for hours on end.

She was sitting in the window seat of the stern

window reading a book she had found and his breath left him at the picture she presented. It was one he always imagined... a lovely wife of his waiting for her husband to return to their cabin. Her hair flowed down her back in a cascade of dark brown curls. She had donned her gown again and it looked a crumbled mess now that it was dry. He noticed she had at least taken advantage of his bed to stay warm, for his shirt was neatly folded and lying on top along with the blanket he had given her. She rose to meet him and rushed to his side.

"You must be freezing, Jasper. Let me take your coat." She helped him out of the oiled coat. "Your cook came up a while ago and left some hot coffee. It should still be warm."

"Thank you, Miranda. Let me get a change of clothes and I'll return directly." He went to the trunk, grabbed a few garments and left to change in another cabin. Once he was dry again, he returned to his quarters.

Miranda quickly crossed to the table to pour him a mug of coffee which she handed to him, insisting he sit at the table so she could set a blanket over his shoulders.

"Mr. Dennison must have been surprised to see you here," he said, watching her face when she blushed, trying to keep his mind off the fact that the buttons of her gown needed to be redone.

She cleared her throat. "Yes..." she barely mumbled, her cheeks flushing an even rosier shade of red that truly became her. "Surprised is an understatement when he saw me in your... errr... bed."

"At least you listened to me for a change. Did you get some rest?" He warmed his hands on the mug of coffee before taking a sip. The hot brew began to work its magic, or perhaps it was the vision before him that was thawing every part of his body. The idea of Miranda sleeping in his bed produced ungentlemanly thoughts. He seemed to lose all sense whenever she was near.

"No, not really," she answered, and her gaze said she truly had been worried about his safety. "I was more concerned with this ship toppling over and whether you were staying safe above deck. What happened, Jasper?"

"The storm and sabotage to the ship." He suppressed his anger and took another sip from his mug, then setting it on the table.

"Who would try to do such a thing?" she gasped.

"We found the culprit, and he's currently locked up in a cell in my hold. We'll interrogate him soon, now that we've ensured all the passengers are safely off the ship, it is well secured so it's not further damaged, and our cargo hasn't been ruined. We've offloaded what was stored on deck in order to allow more room for repairs that are needed topside."

"How horrible someone would try to ruin you in such a way, especially with passengers on board. The loss of life alone would be far greater than the monetary value of whatever you're planning to sell."

"I have an idea who is behind the scheme, but without proof, it's only a hunch." He ran his hand through his wet hair.

"You will be careful, won't you, Jasper?" she asked, taking hold of his hand.

He raised her knuckles to his lips and felt her fingers tremble in his. "Yes, of course, *mademoiselle*," he whispered, running his thumb over her hand before placing a kiss to the inside of her wrist. Her heavenly sigh went straight to his heart. No matter what she claimed, her actions more than told him she cared for him. Why else would she be here aboard his ship?

"I would hate for anything to happen to you, Captain," she murmured, confirming his thoughts. Her voice was like a soft caress over his weary body.

"Miranda..." he began, "we must talk about your presence here."

She jumped up as if she knew what he was about to say. In her nervousness, she began tidying up the cabin, not that there was really much for her to do. She finally stood near the window looking out over the water.

He pushed back his chair and went to her, taking her arms and turning her body into his. He lifted her chin. Pools of tears threatened to escape her eyes and he wished he could take some of her fear away.

"How many saw you being rowed out to my ship?" he asked, already knowing her answer. He had seen for himself how the villagers had come to the aid of his wreck and Jasper was certain Miranda wouldn't have been missed among them.

An unladylike sound erupted from her lips. "Far too many, including Lady Felicity Belvoir and her brother the Earl of Hythe."

"I assume you've been staying at a nearby inn?"

Miranda nodded. "The Queen's Barque. I was lucky to find a room where the roof didn't leak."

"Did others see you rush out into the storm from the inn?" he asked, while skimming his hand over her back. He'd have to do something about those uneven buttons.

"I was having tea with two ladies, but there were more than enough people who also ran to the sound of the bell."

"Maybe you won't be missed then," he said, trying to give her a bit of hope that all was not lost.

"Oh, no!" Her cry rang out in the cabin and she pulled out of his arms.

"What's the matter?" Jasper asked in alarm.

Her lips quivered before she spoke. "There's a rumor circulating at the inn that a reporter from that ghastly *Teatime Tattler* is in residence. If word were to leak to whomever this is that I was here..."

"We'll think of something," he said, but was unprepared when she ran back into his arms. Her head rested upon his chest and he pulled her closer.

"I'm ruined! I've no one to blame but myself for this

mess." Her tears began to soak his shirt and he could only whisper nonsensical words of comfort that really were no comfort whatsoever.

"I'm partly to blame for the situation. I should have sent you back to shore with the next boat instead of indulging my need to keep you safe inside my cabin."

She began shaking her head. "No. You're not to blame at all, Jasper. It was my own stupidity that has my reputation now in tatters."

"We can marry and that will solve all our problems," Jasper replied, thinking of the only solution that would allow this woman to remain at his side. He didn't want to lose her to another.

She once more pulled out of his arms and paced the length of his cabin. "Maybe there is hope! It's almost dark. I can creep up the servant's stairs at the inn and make my way to my room. Surely there must be complete chaos running rampant with all those who were in need of medical care? The inn was already crammed full with guests. I can slip inside with none the wiser," she exclaimed happily.

Jaspar became increasingly dismayed as she rambled on about her plan. "Miranda..."

"Yes, Jasper?" Her eyes twinkled in delight that she had solved her problem.

"Did you hear a word I just said?" he asked, knowing her answer.

Her finger tapped at her lip, drawing attention to the mouth that Jasper desperately wanted to kiss. "Sorry..." she replied, apparently lost in thought. "What did you say?"

"Marry me." His words grounded the woman to a halt and wide eyes stared at him from across the cabin.

"Marry you?" she gasped out, her hand reaching for her throat.

"Yes. Marry me," Jasper replied, with a weak smile.

Harsh laughter escaped her. "I cannot marry you!"

"Why not?"

"And trap us both into a marriage neither of us wants? That's no way to start a life together."

"And yet you'd rather have a life with some titled gent? You think that will bring you the happiness you deserve?" he shouted, furious that she would once again dismiss him as an unsuitable husband.

She pointed her finger at him, anger brimming in her eyes. "Don't you dare judge me, Jasper Rousseau!"

He pulled her into his arms. "I'm not trying to criticize you, Miranda. I'm only trying to understand how you can possibly deny the attraction between us that brought you aboard my ship in the first place."

"It was impulsive," she whispered. "A mistake."

"We are not a mistake."

"We are!"

"No, we are not, and I'll prove it to you," Jasper declared, as he once again lifted her chin to meet his eyes.

Bending down, his lips brushed against her mouth, coaxing her to join him in this crazy connection they had between them. His hand came to rest on her cheek and when she leaned into his hand, all her inhibitions seemingly left her. She molded herself into his body while her arms wound themselves around his neck. His tongue skimmed along the seam of her lips and when they parted to allow his tongue to dance with her own, a moan escaped her. He took possession of her, laying a claim that he hoped no one had dared before. Miranda was his and he swore he would convince her that they were a perfect match for one another.

Minutes passed but the world could have swept them away and Jasper wouldn't have cared if time became hours. But with those thoughts also came the fact that he needed to help Miranda salvage her reputation to the best of his ability. He ended their kiss. Their mouths hovered next to each other as their breaths became one. He finally kissed her forehead, holding her at arms-length. When she gazed up at him in wonder, he also prayed that perhaps she had seen reason in his offer.

"Lie to yourself, if you wish, Miranda, but I know the truth of the matter. You care for me or you never would have risked everything to learn of my welfare."

He claimed her lips in one last searing kiss before he turned her around and began redoing the buttons of her gown. Once he was finished, he grabbed the oiled coat she had arrived in while she quickly made an attempt at fixing her hair. She failed, miserably, and only appeared more than ever as if she had taken a recent tumble in his bed. Considering her lips were redder from his kiss, she never looked more lovely.

She headed for the door to the cabin as fast as her feet would take her. "Good-bye, Jasper," she tossed over her shoulder.

He followed close behind. "Only for now, *mon amour*," Jasper murmured before running a finger down her cheek.

"You c-cannot p-possibly think you're g-going to accompany me," she sputtered.

"I will see you back to the inn. This is *not* up for negotiation," Jasper warned.

"I hardly think that is necessary, Jasper," she said, obviously trying to persuade him to change his mind.

"I'll leave you at the inn, but this matter between us is in no way settled. We will talk again, although our conversation may be delayed a few days while repairs are being made to my ship."

For once, she didn't argue with him, and Jasper wasn't positive that a quiet Miranda was better than one who was fighting with him. For now, he let the matter rest.

Under the cover of night, they made their way down off his ship to the skiff that was tied alongside *The Legacy*. Now that the worst of the storm had passed, rowing across the harbor was easier than when Miranda had arrived. The trip over the dunes and back to the inn took less time than he would have liked and with a hasty farewell, Miranda disappeared inside the Queen's Barque.

Jasper could only reluctantly let her go. He would need to trust his instincts about the feelings he knew they had for one another. He prayed what he thought they had wasn't all one sided.

CHAPTER 12

G etting ready for the excursion to the church the next day, Miranda stared at her reflection in the mirror. Did she appear any different than she had a day ago before her world turned upside down? She could no longer dismiss her feelings for Jasper. They had grown into a burning flame. He had offered marriage to save her reputation. She was ruined but she was glad she'd gone to check on his safety.

She had thought her flight up the servants' stairs last evening a brilliant idea. But she had only ascended half way up when she bumped into a maid. Old newsprints went spilling from the girl's hands and they both quickly reached down to gather them. Miranda had held back her surprise when she realized she was collecting old editions of *The Teatime Tattler*. Praying her name wasn't linked to anything inside that gossip rag, Miranda handed her copies to the girl. A gleam of satisfaction briefly flickered in the maid's eyes. Miranda left, mumbling her apologies, and her feet flew to her room, where she remained in hiding the rest of the evening.

But Miranda was not going to stay closeted away cowering like some skittish colt. No! She would face whatever she must, however Society might ostracize her. She had recovered from more than one outlandish stain upon her reputation. This would be no different.

Elsie finished arranging Miranda's hair for the outing to the church and, after grabbing her shawl, Miranda made her way down to the reception room where she found the other ladies assembled for their trip through the village.

"I'm delighted everyone could join us. Allow me to introduce Lady Felicity Belvoir," Miranda announced, gesturing to the young woman standing next to her. "We wait only for Mr. Somerville, the village vicar, to arrive before departing."

Other introductions were made to those who were unknown to each other in the party, including Miss Verity Walford who was Eugenia's traveling companion. Miranda nodded politely and they conversed until the door opened. Mr. Somerville and another gentleman named Mr. Gilroy entered and were also introduced.

"Ah, Miss de Courtenay. What a pleasure to meet you." Gilroy beamed at Miranda taking her hand and bowing over it. "You and your friends are about to visit the church, if what Mr. Somerville tells me is correct."

Miranda was never one to turn down attention from an attractive man. "We are, sir."

"It's vastly unfair that Somerville alone is privileged to enjoy the company of so many fair damsels. Might I be your escort as well?" He offered his arm to Miranda and Verity.

"By all means," Verity said, murmuring her thanks.

Eugenia turned to Mr. Somerville. "I'm so looking forward to seeing the church and learning its history."

The man offered his arm to her and extended his other to Lady Felicity. "I'm honored by the interest of all of you ladies. Mrs. Brewster has undoubtedly explained that the church, like the Queen's Barque, was visited by Her Majesty Queen Elizabeth, who gifted it a window. In my view, its surviving Norman features are even more fascinating. I'll explain more when we arrive at the sanctuary. Ladies, are you all ready to depart?"

Everyone agreed and they went outside to a day full of sunshine, despite the mud underfoot and the scudding clouds. The walk to the church didn't take long before they entered a beautifully preserved example of Norman architecture.

Mr. Somerville began explaining the details. "The stained-glass rosette window was a gift from Queen Elizabeth. You'll note, from that queen's coat of arms, the lion and dragon rampant in the two lower corners as well as the triple Fleur de Lis and lions supine in the upper corners."

Although the church was indeed impressive,

Miranda lost all interest in the description that kept the other ladies entertained until the door opened and Lord Danville rushed inside. Miranda stood her ground as he began making his way toward her. How strange was it that she was no longer excited to see him?

"What a pleasant surprise to see you here, Lord Danville," Miranda murmured, while he bowed over the hand that she extended him. Even though she had wanted to see what could possibly become of a relationship with him at one point during this journey, there was another that her heart continued to long for. The way she felt about Jasper altered everything she used to want in her life. A possible relationship with Lord Danville no longer held any appeal.

"I just learned your group was meeting here and I hurried over to see if I might join everyone and enjoy your lovely company," Danville replied. A hopeful expression flickered within his eyes.

"You are too kind, Lord Danville. As you can see, we are quite the group today." She waved her hand towards the others who continued to listen to Mr. Somerville. "You are more than welcome to join us."

He tucked her hand into the crook of his arm. "If I am honest, I'm really only here to spend time with you, dear lady. I missed seeing your return to the taproom last evening," he began while intently watching her face. "I hope all is well."

"Y-yes, of course. I-I just thought I might be coming down with a cold after being out in the rain helping those who were in need. I decided it was best to keep to my room," she stammered, while returning her attention to the others.

"Understandable. I must admit I was very concerned when you rushed out into the storm. Very noble of you to wish to help with those who were shipwrecked," he said but there was something in his eyes that made Miranda hold back a further reply referencing Jasper.

Instead she turned the conversation away from herself. "I am surprised to see you here in Fenwick on Sea, Lord Danville. The last we talked at the coaching inn, your business was in Yarmouth where your ship was docked."

His eyes narrowed before he quickly transformed his features with a smile that didn't quite each his eyes "A last minute change in plans left me stranded with the rest of the occupants of the Queen's Barque due to the flooded roads. Sometimes my business takes me to places where I don't normally trade. An occupational necessity. My schedule adapts accordingly to the needs of my business, my dear."

His endearment left Miranda with a cold dread in the pit of her stomach. Something was strange with the man before her. Something she hadn't felt when she had met him but days before. Or perhaps it was Miranda herself who had changed. In either case, for once she listened to her inner voice to not encourage any further attention from Danville or indulge in speculations about a future with him.

"I'm certain your shipping trade takes you all over the world," she replied, while trying to disengage her hand from his elbow. He held firm and, unless she wanted to make a scene in a church, she let the matter rest for now. "Now that the storm has passed, I assume you'll be leaving for Yarmouth shortly."

"My business should conclude in the next couple of days. Will you be leaving soon as well?" he asked pulling her closer to his side.

"Yes. I will continue on my journey as soon as the coach is fixed. The driver said the blacksmith here in the village should have it repaired soon."

"Marvelous! We can continue to enjoy each other's company at the inn until our departures," he beamed, with a bright smile.

Before she could answer, their group began leaving the church and she had no choice but to continue to allow Hugo to escort her through the short tour of the rest of the village.

When they returned to the inn, Mrs. Brewster had tea waiting for them and they all took seats at a large table. Conversations swarmed around the crowded room and Miranda sat quietly sipping her tea, not really wishing to make idle chit chat, trying to ignore Lord Danville who insisted on sitting next to her. But when a tall form filled the entryway to the room, her eyes lit up in excitement for the first time that day.

Jasper had arrived, but he hardly looked happy to see her. Whatever was the matter with him now?

When Jasper saw Miranda sitting next to Hugo Danville, fire erupted in his veins. What the bloody hell was she doing with his enemy? Not that she knew the rivalry between their families, but hostility suddenly overwhelmed him at seeing them together. He took a deep breath and reassured himself he was overreacting. She was sitting at a table with more than enough people that she could call for help if the need arose.

Seeing Danville was a grim reminder Jasper still had to deal with the crewman he had in his hold. Jasper had been so occupied with the needed repairs to his ship, that he had delayed the needed interrogation. He would rectify that soon.

He gave a brief nod of his head to the lady who had consumed his thoughts since he had last seen her. She excused herself from the table and made her way across the room. She gave a short curtsey and he bowed before she held out her hand. The moment he took her fingertips within his own, those same crazy currents raced up his arm. He kissed the air between his lips and her hand, knowing they had the attention of the room.

"You look lovely today, Miss de Courtenay," Jasper said, knowing the need to keep up appearances for the sake of the others.

"You are too kind, Captain Rousseau," she answered. The smile she bestowed upon him set his heart lurching in his chest, making him forget his anger of but moments ago.

"Might we have a private word, Miranda?" he asked quietly.

"I don't see how that's possible, Jasper," she responded softly, "not when there are so many watching us."

"Then let us sit over at the table by the hearth," he said, pointing across the room to the vacant chairs. "We'll still be in the company of others but far enough away where we won't be overheard."

"That should be acceptable," she agreed.

Jasper led her to the table and a maid came with another pot of tea for them to share. She briefly lingered at their table before taking her leave. After Miranda had poured and handed him a cup, Jasper couldn't hold back his concern. "I've been worried whether you were able to get to your room last night unnoticed."

"I'm afraid not," Miranda replied, discreetly nodding to the servant who just left. "I ran into the maid who just served us but there's no need to worry about that now. There's nothing I can do about what happened at this point, and I'll make my excuses to my brother and sister when I return home, if the need arises."

"I'm sorry for the trouble this has caused you," Jasper replied, before his gaze returned to his nemesis across the room. "It may not be any of my business, Miranda, but how do you know Hugo Danville?"

Miranda set her cup down. "You mean Lord Danville?"

Jasper jerked taller in his chair. Cursing beneath his breath, he glared at her. "*Lord?* Is that how he's passing himself off these days?"

Their glances across the room showed Hugo was intently watching them. "He's not titled?"

"Hardly. He and his father have made their money in trade, mostly from the black market. He doesn't move in respectable circles, which is why I was concerned when I saw you seated next to him. How did you meet?"

"At a coaching inn on my way here. He introduced himself, but I was surprised to see him here in Fenwick on Sea, since he had not mentioned his business would take him south. At the time, I will admit, I thought him charming."

"He can put on a convincing façade, *ma chérie*. I can only advise, based on my past relationship with him, that you would do well to stay as far away from him as possible. He can be dangerous, and I would know, since he has been trying to ruin my business for years," Jasper confided.

"You cannot be serious," she gasped.

"I'm afraid so. It's an old rivalry between our families and I think Danville will do anything to further our ruin. I already believe he is the person responsible for the recent accidents that happened on *The Legacy*. We have someone in custody but have yet to question the man. I won't be surprised to learn that Danville paid the man to do so much damage."

"I'll be careful, Jasper," she responded, a frown marring her brow. "Besides, I won't be here much longer and see no reason why I would further any sort of association with him. The coach should be repaired in the next couple of days and I understand the roads should be passable by then. I can then be on my way to stay with Lady Jane before returning to Grace and Nicholas's cottage in Cromer."

"Will you be at your friend's long?" he asked, wondering when he would be able to see her again.

"She should have her child any day now; that is the reason why I was in such a hurry to reach her home. I never expected to be stranded here in Fenwick on Sea for so many days," she replied, searching his eyes. He briefly wondered if she were thinking the same thoughts he had just moments ago.

"The storm has been most unfortunate."

"How are the repairs to your ship going?" she asked, confirming that her thoughts matched with his.

"Better than expected, thanks in part to the fact *The Legacy* has been blocking the entire harbor. With the villagers' help, along with my own crew, she should be refloated shortly and we can finish the remainder of the repairs with her out of the way of other shipping."

"And where are you sailing next?" she inquired, before taking a sip of her tea. "I'll be honest and say I didn't pay any attention when I was onboard previously, when you gave us a tour of your vessel."

"Ostend in the Low Country to drop off passengers. I then have other business there that will have me in port for a while.

She gave a heavy sigh. "Then it will be some time before you return to England." She looked so forlorn it about broke Jasper's heart.

He reached across the table to take her hand, despite the audience they had. "Will you miss me," he teased, with a coaxing smile. When sudden laughter burst from her lips, Jasper glowed at the thought he was the cause of her joy. In that instant, he fell more in love with this woman before him.

"I would never admit such to you, Jasper, even if I did. A woman does need a bit of mystery or two about her. How else would she keep a gentleman interested in returning for her?" She looked at him shyly. "You will come back... for me? Won't you, Jasper?"

"You must know I will, Miranda." His husky reply had her blushing.

"I shall look forward to our reunion at some later date."

"Then you'll wait for me?" he asked, hopefully. "No more of this business of wanting some titled gentleman for a husband?"

She stood and offered her hand to him and he once more bowed over it. "You'll have the task of getting my brother to give his blessing first. If you can manage such a feat, then I'll be waiting and our reunion will be all the sweeter."

She mumbled her thanks for the tea and returned to her original party.

As Jasper made his way back to his ship, he began to wonder how many more times he would have to say goodbye to the lovely Miranda.

CHAPTER 13

I n the next few days, Miranda managed to have two
short and frustrating encounters in the public
parlor of the inn with Jasper, when he had reason to
come ashore, and to avoid more than the briefest of
conversations with Hugo Danville.

Friday morning dawned bright and clear and, after a
light breakfast, Miranda and Elsie enjoyed a stroll along
the beach. Miranda had learned the coach had been
repaired and they would finally leave the Queen's
Barque by early afternoon so they could reach their
destination with plenty of daylight.

In many ways, Miranda would miss this brief
reprieve from the restrictions of her daily life. She had
found a certain amount of freedom while she had been
stranded in this tiny fishing village near the sea. With
the roads opened again, she would return to her normal
life and the possible repercussions from any reports in

the *Teatime Tattler* of her wild dash to the wreck and her late return to the inn. She could only move forward at this point. There was no changing the past. She would deal with the scorn of Society when she must.

Miranda understood why her moments with Jasper had been so constrained. After all, he was behind his deadline for getting his passengers and cargo delivered, not that it was his fault his ship had become damaged in the storm. But she reasoned that such a delay was hardly good for business, whether he was to blame or not. However, she couldn't resist the urge to have one last look at the man who had stolen her heart, even if it was from the distance of the harbor.

The chore of getting *The Legacy* released from the rocky shoal had been completed, and the ship now lightly bobbed up and down in the gentle waves of the inlet instead of blocking its entrance. Miranda had learned from those who returned to the inn that there had been no damage to its hull, so at least that wasn't something else Jasper had to worry over. The other ships that had taken refuge from the storm could now embark for their original destinations.

From the distance, she watched men climb the rigging as they went about their work, including those who hung from the rear of the ship while they repaired the rudder chain. Shielding her eyes from the sun, she couldn't imagine the courage it must take to climb such dizzying heights. Still... her eyes searched for the one man among many who had crept into her heart when she least expected it. Who would have thought she could come to care for a man so easily or so quickly? They barely knew one another and yet Miranda felt as though Jasper had always been a part of her life, no matter how insane that sounded.

He came to the railing and waved when he recognized her, and she returned the gesture until he once more disappeared to return to his duties. She would miss him terribly, and she continued to ponder how he had made such a claim upon her heart. Miranda only knew Jasper had completely turned her way of thinking. A silly title now seemed so insignificant compared to having someone's love... no... not just anyone's love. It was Jasper's love that had changed her. He made the difference the moment he found her in Bath months ago.

Time was getting away from them. Miranda and Elsie walked back towards the inn. When she saw Hugo emerge from a building with a group of men, she frowned, wondering what he was doing. But it was none of her business, and she would heed Jasper's warning to beware of the man.

Unfortunately, Hugo had other plans, for he ran to catch up with her and forcefully took her arm. "Why, if it isn't Rousseau's little chit," he sneered, no longer keeping up any pretense. "I had thought you all prim and proper but rumors going around the Queen's Barque tell me differently." He began pulling her down the lane toward a carriage waiting near the inn.

"How dare you talk to me like that? Get your filthy hands off me this instant," she fumed, trying to loosen his grip to no avail.

"You're coming with me and, if you know what's good for you, you'll keep your damn mouth shut," he warned, pulling harder on her arm.

"I'm not going anywhere with you," Miranda shouted, but began to panic when she realized Hugo was far too strong. No matter what she did, she was at his mercy.

Elsie began trying to claw his fingers from around Miranda's arm. "You let her go this instant!"

Her poor maid didn't see the backhand landing on her cheek, sending the dazed girl tumbling to the ground. As the two women became further and further apart, Elsie's eyes widened in fright.

"Elsie! Run and get help," Miranda yelled out, when her maid was at last able to pick herself up from the ground and dash away.

"Bloody hell," Hugo cursed, as he continued to drag Miranda toward a waiting carriage. When they reached it, he pulled open the door and tossed Miranda inside. She had barely gathered her feet beneath her and was about to open the opposite door, when Hugo jumped inside and took hold of her wrists, tying them together with a rope. He then rapped on the roof and the carriage took off, even as Miranda let out a scream of protest.

"Why are you doing this?" she cried out when she saw his plans to gag her next.

"Isn't it obvious, my pet?" His smile was completely wicked as he put the rag in place so she couldn't answer him. "Rousseau wants you. There's no better reason than that for me to steal you away so he can never have you."

His laughter rang out in the carriage, and deep cold dread consumed Miranda. Only a miracle could save her now from the madman who held her captive.

CHAPTER 14

J asper watched as the crewman who had been held prisoner was tied to one of the masts. The man had confessed more than Jasper had hoped, including his association with Danville, who had hired him to sabotage the ship. Jasper now had proof about how far his enemy would go to cause havoc in Jasper's business. He had found it hard to believe that Hugo would put innocent passengers in jeopardy. The man was even worse than Jasper had believed.

"Mr. Watson," Jasper called, before nodding to his Quartermaster who unfurled a whip at his side. "See that a swift punishment is given before returning this scum to the hold. As soon as we return to London, we'll see that he makes his confession to the local magistrate."

"Aye, Captain," the man said, before the crack of the whip sounded out. Any of the crew who might be tempted to take payment from an enemy in future needed to know what was in store for a traitor.

Jasper heard a shout from the shore. A woman was waving her arms. Alarm froze his face when he recognized her. She had been with Miranda a short while ago.

"Gasparel," Jasper shouted out to his long-time friend before heading toward the railing and a skiff waiting below. "You're in charge until I return."

"What's the matter? I thought we were getting ready to sail."

Jasper pointed in the direction of the shore. "I have a feeling something is wrong with Miranda, and Danville may be the cause of it."

"Here," Gasparel spat, thrusting a pistol at Jasper. "Don't go without something to defend yourself."

Jasper nodded his thanks. He descended the ladder and was soon rowing over to the shore. The closer he got to land, the more frantic the woman became as tears cascaded freely down her cheeks.

"Thank God, Captain Rousseau! You must save Miss de Courtenay," she exclaimed.

Jasper gently took hold of the woman's chin, seeing the red bruise already forming on her cheek. "Who did this to you, Miss?" he asked already knowing her answer.

"It was that horrible man we met in Norwich... Lord Danville. He dragged Miss de Courtenay into a carriage," she began to cry in earnest. "You must save her!"

"You can trust that I will do all in my power to return her safe and sound," Jasper replied, before breaking out into a run, pulling her by the hand. He headed toward the Queen's Barque and burst inside demanding a horse. He impatiently waited in the courtyard while the steed was saddled.

Man and beast became one as Jasper pushed the horse into a gallop in order to catch up with the carriage that had taken Miranda away. He could quickly gain ground, since he would be able to ride faster than a carriage could travel. As long as he was going the right way. Danville had boasted his ship was anchored at Yarmouth; Jasper could only hope they were headed in that direction.

He was relieved to see the outline of the conveyance up ahead of him. Leaning over the steed's neck, he flicked the reins, causing the animal to lurch forward. As he came abreast of the carriage, he peered inside to see Miranda bound and gagged. Anger flooded his veins and, as he came in line with the driver, he pulled out the pistol yelling at the man to stop.

With the team of horses lurching to a halt, a growl of outrage came from inside the carriage. The door was flung open and Danville threw himself at Jasper who lost his grip on the pistol. The two men landed in the dirt and began fighting fist to fist until Danville pulled out a knife. Jasper watched the blade being tossed from hand to hand.

Danville called out to the driver of the coach. "Shoot him!"

"Nothing to do with me, guv. You gents sort it out yourselves."

"I enjoyed taking your little toy away from you, Rousseau," Danville taunted. "She'll make a good whore on some tropical island far from your reach once I sell her to the highest bidder. I'll look forward to the coins that will line my purse with her purchase!"

"You're threatening the woman I care for, Danville. Your reputation with the women you abuse is finally catching up with you. You won't be selling them any longer now that Miss de Courtenay is a witness to your plans for her. I knew you made your money from the black market, but this is despicable, even for you."

"You bastard!" Danville yelled taking a swipe with the blade. "I'll kill you and spit on your dead body afterwards."

"And I'll look forward to seeing you put in jail for what you've done to the young lady and also for the damage you've caused on my ship," Jasper said, and enjoyed the brief flicker of fear in Hugo's eyes.

The two men circled one another. Jasper lunged towards his enemy and was able to knock the knife from Danville's grasp. They once more began throwing punches. Jasper made every attempt to keep his attention on his enemy despite catching a glimpse of Miranda emerging from the coach. She had managed to somehow untie the ropes that had held her captive and was racing toward the pistol.

Danville had just taken hold of the knife and raised his arm to flick the weapon at Jasper when the sound of the pistol rang out. The blade fell from his hand as he fell to the ground. Miranda stood there holding the smoking gun, with a gleam of satisfaction on her face.

"That bloody bitch shot me in the leg," Hugo complained, holding his injured thigh, unable to do more than moan and thrash.

"You're lucky I didn't shoot you directly in your black heart!" she called out, before she flung herself into Jasper's waiting arms.

"You saved me," he said, taking her cheeks in his hands and examining her for injuries.

"I think we saved each other," she confessed, before kissing him.

"Where on earth did you learn how to shoot a pistol?" Jasper asked.

Miranda gave a hesitant shrug. "My brother gave both Grace and me lessons just in case we ever had need to defend ourselves."

"Smart brother."

Miranda gave a short laugh. "He would agree with you."

"Remind me to thank him when next we meet," he replied.

Jasper gave her a quick hug before taking the discarded rope and tying Hugo up to take to the local magistrate. Jasper would give testimony of what happened and the rest of Hugo's fate would be out of his hands.

Jasper ordered the carriage to return to Fenwick on Sea with Danville secured inside. There was no way he was going to ask Miranda to share the carriage with the snake, bound or not. He jumped into his saddle and held out his hands for his lady. He settled her into his lap and she rested her head upon his shoulder as they made their way back to the inn.

There was quite the ruckus when they returned, since Miranda's maid had alerted everyone about what had happened. Jasper escorted Miranda inside but was surprised when she swept her arms around his neck in a fierce hug.

"You realize your reputation is going to be ruined even further than it was before, *mon amour*, after such a display of affection," Jasper whispered into her ear while keeping her close.

"I couldn't care a fig what they think of me," she replied tartly, before lifting her chin and pursing her lips to receive his kiss.

Never one to leave a lady wanting, he gave free expression to the desire he had been holding in. She was his... they belonged forever together.

CHAPTER 15

Cromer, England
Three Months Later

Miranda sat next to a large picture window staring out over the sea in her sister's cottage. Nicholas's daughter Blanche and his and Grace's baby boy played on a blanket on the floor, making Miranda wish for a child of her own one day... that was if she were ever to marry. She had almost given up on Jasper's return after only three months. How would she ever survive waiting on shore for months on end while her husband was at sea?

"He'll be here soon," Grace said, as if reading her mind. She poured a cup of tea, handing the porcelain to Miranda.

"I wish he was here now," Miranda confessed, with a

smile that swiftly faded. Had the man she had come to love forgotten about her?

"Stop it," Grace ordered while her eyes lit up in a mischievous twinkle.

"Stop what?" Miranda asked, not knowing what her sister was talking about.

"Stop thinking Jasper isn't going to return. He loves you. Just be patient."

Miranda laughed. "You, above all people, should know being patient is not one of my strong points."

"Should we place a bet then?" Grace smirked with a knowing grin.

"Our betting days are over, Gracie," Miranda said throwing up her hands. "I've learned my lesson."

"If you're certain..." Grace let the challenge hang in the air.

"I am," Miranda answered, setting down her cup before following Grace's gaze out the window. A lone gentleman was walking along the shore and as he came closer, recognition lit Miranda's face. "He's here!

"Well, go on then. Don't keep your man waiting for you," Grace urged. Miranda ran from the house, down the back stairs and out onto the sand.

She had never been so happy to see anyone in her life and, when Jasper recognized her, he also began running. If she had been paying better attention, she would have seen Jasper's ship anchored off the shoreline just as Grace had.

"Jasper," she called out, before she jumped into his arms. He began twirling her around and around on the sand.

"Miranda!" he rejoiced before setting her down on her feet. "How I have missed you."

He bent down and his lips touched her own. Miranda wanted nothing more than their kiss to last forever more. She gave everything she had into their kiss leaving him no doubt how much he had been missed.

They began walking along the shoreline hand in hand before she raised questioning eyes up to him. "What took you so long?" she asked quietly. "I thought you would have been here before now."

"It's your brother's fault, actually," Jasper began. "Took me forever to track down his whereabouts. I finally found him up at his manor in Saltford."

"You asked for his blessing?"

"Yes." Jasper stole another kiss before they continued their stroll. "You told me I had to."

"And are you going to tell me his answer?"

"He gave it after I told him that there would never be another man who would love you as deeply as I love you," Jasper answered, taking her hand and kissing the inside of her wrist.

"You love me," she sighed, tears forming in her eyes.

He leaned down to whisper in her ear. "This is the part where you tell me you love me too, *ma petite.*"

"Oh Jasper! I do love you, more than you'll ever know," she exclaimed, and, for the first time in her life, she knew what it was to be truly happy.

"Then would you do me the honor of becoming my wife?" he asked, pulling out a ring from his jacket.

Miranda stared at the square cut emerald surrounded by tiny diamonds. "Yes, Jasper," she replied. "I would be honored to become your wife."

He placed the ring upon her finger. Brushing the tears that began to run down her cheeks, he once more placed his lips upon her own. "I hope those are happy tears, *mon amour*," Jasper replied.

"Of course, they are. I'm only saddened thinking of the months we'll spend apart while you travel and I'm left on shore," Miranda answered, trying not to cloud this moment she had been waiting for all her life.

"Leave you on shore? You must be crazy if you think I'll leave you on shore when I can have my lovely wife with me each and every day," Jasper declared before lifting her up and swinging her around again.

"You mean I can travel with you?" she asked, while bursts of happiness poured from her eyes.

"I wouldn't have it any other way, my lovely lady. Life with you, Miranda, will be one hell of an adventure!" Jasper laughed before kissing her again.

When they entered Grace's home and Nicholas poured champagne to celebrate their announcement, Miranda could only stare in wonder at the man who had changed her world. Thanks to him, she had opened her eyes to see the person, not the title or the money, and finally fallen in love. Jasper was right... she'd never have a dull moment as long as Jasper was her husband. She would look forward to their journey through the rest of their lives together.

EPILOGUE

The Caribbean Sea
One Year Later

J asper held his tiny infant son in his arms while he made his way to the bow of his ship. His beautiful wife stood there much as she had done over a year ago in London, before she was his. This time, though, her dark brown hair was free of its normal restraints and floated on the ocean breeze in a heavenly display of curls. She was meant for life at sea and the whole world awaited them as they traveled to new locations in order to fulfill their thirst for new discoveries.

Miranda must have felt his presence, for she turned and opened her arms inviting Jasper and their son to join her at the rail. The crystal-clear blue-green water of the ocean sparkled like diamonds, much like Miranda's eyes did each day they were together.

"He just woke up?" she asked, holding out a finger for the baby to play, only to find the child closing his eyes to doze off again.

"Obviously, he didn't care for my sparkling conversation," Jasper replied, before his mother came over to take the child to coo over him. He didn't mind. It gave him the extra opportunity to be alone with his wife.

"I never knew I could be so happy, Jasper," Miranda murmured, turning in his arms to face him. "I adore our life together."

"Before I found you, Miranda, I had never met anyone whom I thought would make me truly happy. You changed all that from the very first moment I saw you upon the dance floor. I know you felt it, too, even though you were too stubborn to admit it."

"You're not trying to pick a fight with me, are you, my darling husband?" she teased with twinkling eyes.

"I would never dare," he laughed, bringing her closer and kissing the top of her head.

"I tried to deny what has been happening between us, Jasper," she confided with a warm smile. "I was so blinded all those years and wasted so much time looking for a titled gentleman to wed, but none of them would have made me happy."

"You were just waiting for me, *mon amour*," he whispered. "I adore you."

"Yes, I was. I'm so glad you found me, Jasper. You must know how very much I love you," she murmured.

"Show me," he said, as he began nibbling at her ear.

"In the middle of the day?" she gasped out, before looking around the deck. For once, the crew seemed to have vanished—including Jasper's parents, much to his delight.

A chuckle escaped him when he saw how embarrassed she appeared. "Has that ever stopped us before?"

She giggled. "Well... now that you mention it, it hasn't. What did you have in mind?"

"I'm certain you will think of something, my beautiful wife," he replied with a roguish grin, as he led her down to their cabin.

And she did... on that day and for many years to come Miranda showered Jasper with so much love he never once regretted making her his wife. Something this strong would surely last beyond this lifetime and extend until the end of time itself. For Jasper, he couldn't ask for anything more from the love he shared with his wife. Life with Miranda was indeed a grand adventure!

The End

Sherry Ewing needs your help!

Book reviews help readers to find books, and authors to find readers. Please consider writing a review for ***Before I Found You***, even a couple of sentences telling people what you liked (or didn't like) about the stories. Reviews can be posted on BookBub, Goodreads, and on most eRetailers websites. For links to this book on those sites, see my website at https://sherryewing.com/books/before-i-found-you-2/

I really appreciate the time you take to write your reviews and, yes, I read them all! Thank you for purchasing a copy of *Before I Found You*. I hope you've enjoyed Jasper and Miranda's journey to finding love!

AUTHOR'S NOTE

Thank you, dearest readers, for purchasing a copy of *Before I Found You*. I hope you enjoyed Miranda's happily-ever-after!

Miranda made her first appearance in *A Kiss For Charity* followed by *The Earl Takes A Wife*. As her character developed, I knew it would take a special hero for her to learn what truly mattered in life. I believe Jasper was just who she needed.

Thank you to the Bluestocking Belles who played an important role in Miranda's development over the years. She has come a long way and I am thankful to the Belles who allowed her to be featured in their novellas.

Elisabeth Essex was willing to share her wealth of information relating to Jasper's ship and everything nautical. It's authors like her that are willing to help out another author that makes this business so enjoyable. Thank you, Elizabeth!

A special thank you to my street and review teams. Your support means the world to me and I appreciate everything you do on my behalf!

If you enjoyed Miranda and Jasper's story, please consider writing a review. Even a few words will help so other readers can find my work. You can also learn more about my Regency, medieval, and time travel stories on my website at https://www.sherryewing.com/books.

Keep an eye out for my next release *Promises Made At Midnight: The Knights of Berwyck, A Quest Through Time (Book Six)* to be released July 2022. I know you're going to love it!

Until the next time, I look forward to seeing your posts on our mutual social media outlets.

All the best,
   Sherry Ewing

OTHER BOOKS BY SHERRY EWING

Medieval & Time Travel Series

To Love A Scottish Laird: De Wolfe Pack Connected World

Sometimes you really can fall in love at first sight...

To Love An English Knight: De Wolfe Pack Connected World

Can a chance encounter lead to love?

If My Heart Could See You: The MacLarens, A Medieval Romance (Book One)

When you're enemies, does love have a fighting chance?

For All of Ever: The Knights of Berwyck, A Quest Through Time (Book One)

Sometimes to find your future, you must look to the past...

Only For You: The Knights of Berwyck, A Quest Through Time (Book Two)

Sometimes it's hard to remember that true love conquers all, only after the battle is over...

Hearts Across Time: The Knights of Berwyck (Books One & Two)

Sometimes all you need is to just believe... Hearts Across Time is a special edition box set that combines Katherine and Riorden's stories together from *For All of Ever* and *Only For You*.

A Knight To Call My Own: The MacLarens, A Medieval Romance (Book Two)

When your heart is broken, is love still worth the risk?

To Follow My Heart: The Knights of Berwyck, A Quest Through Time (Book Three)

Love is a leap. Sometimes you need to jump...

The Piper's Lady: The MacLarens, A Medieval Romance (Book Three)

True love binds them. Deceit divides them. Will they choose love?

Love Will Find You: The Knights of Berwyck, A Quest Through Time (Book Four)

Sometimes a moment is all we have...

One Last Kiss: The Knights of Berwyck, A Quest Through Time (Book Five)

Sometimes it takes a miracle to find your heart's desire...

Promises Made At Midnight: The Knights of Berwyck, A Quest Through Time (Book Six)

Make a wish...

Regency

A Kiss For Charity: A de Courtenay Novella (Book One)

Love heals all wounds but will their pride keep them apart?

The Earl Takes A Wife: A de Courtenay Novella (Book Two)

It began with a memory, etched in the heart.

Before I Found You: A de Courtenay Novella (Book Three)

A quest for a title. An encounter with a stranger. Will she choose love?

Nothing But Time: A Family of Worth (Book One)

They will risk everything for their forbidden love...

One Moment In Time: A Family of Worth (Book Two)

One moment in time may be enough, if it lasts forever...

Under the Mistletoe

A new suitor seeks her hand. An old flame holds her heart. Which one will she meet under the kissing bough?

A Second Chance At Love

Can the bittersweet frost of lost love be rekindled into a burning flame?

A Countess to Remember in *Desperate Daughters: A Bluestocking Belles with Friends Collection*

You can find out more about Sherry's work on her website at www.SherryEwing.com and at online retailers.

SOCIAL MEDIA

Website: www.SherryEwing.com
Email: Sherry@SherryEwing.com
Bluestocking Belles: www.bluestockingbelles.net/
Amazon Author Page: http://amzn.to/1TrWtoy
Bookbub: www.bookbub.com/authors/sherry-ewing
Facebook: www.Facebook.com/SherryEwingAuthor
Goodreads: www.Goodreads.com/author/show/
8382315.Sherry_Ewing
Instagram: https://instagram.com/sherry.ewing
Pinterest: www.Pinterest.com/SherryLEwing
TikTok: https://www.tiktok.com/@sherryewingauthor
Tumblr: https://sherryewing.tumblr.com
Twitter: www.Twitter.com/Sherry_Ewing
YouTube: http://www.youtube.com/SherryEwingauthor

Sign Me Up!
Newsletter: http://bit.ly/2vGrqQM
Facebook Street Team:
www.facebook.com/groups/799623313455472/
Facebook Official Fan page: https://www.facebook.com/
groups/356905935241836/

ABOUT SHERRY EWING

Sherry Ewing picked up her first historical romance when she was a teenager and has been hooked ever since. A bestselling author, she writes historical and time travel romances to awaken the soul one heart at a time. When not writing, she can be found in the San Francisco area at her day job as an Information Technology Specialist. You can learn more about Sherry on her website where a new adventure awaits you on every page.

Learn more about Sherry at:
Email: Sherry@SherryEwing.com
Newsletter: http://bit.ly/2vGrqQM
Facebook Street Team: https://www.facebook.com/groups/799623313455472/
Facebook Official Fan page: https://www.facebook.com/groups/356905935241836/

www.ingramcontent.com/pod-product-compliance
Lightning Source LLC
Chambersburg PA
CBHW030231180626
46810CB00008B/3078